Summer Storm

A UFC ROMANTIC COMEDY

BLAIR MONROY

AF435471

Books by Blair Monroy

GIRL FIGHT SERIES

Girl Fight

Spring Blues

Summer Storm

Autumn Falling

To my readers. Thank you.

Playlist

EVA'S

SUMMERTIME HIGHTIME | CUCO

CASUAL | CHAPPELL ROAN

EVERYTHING SHE AIN'T | HAILEY WHITTERS

WOLVES | SELENA GOMEZ

YOUR LOVE'S LIKE | SABRINA CARPENTER

YOUNG AND BEAUTIFUL | LANA DEL REY

I MISS YOU | BEYONCE

ERIC'S

SEÑORITA | SHAWN MENDES

PERFECT | ED SHEERAN

HOME | EDWARD SHARP AND THE MAGNETIC ZEROS

WITH ME | SUM 41

YELLOW | COLDPLAY

DONTMAKEMEFALLINLOVE | CUCO

STILL INTO YOU | PARAMORE

CHAPTER

ONE

SCORCHING.

Not "oh, isn't it a bit warm?" scorching. Not "maybe I'll fan myself with a napkin" scorching. No, this was *Satan's armpit hosting a Bikram yoga retreat* scorching. My car—a 2015 relic I've affectionately dubbed The Green Toaster—was living up to its name. The AC wheezed like an asthmatic hamster on a Peloton, blowing air that felt like a hairdryer set to *apocalypse*. By the time I pulled into Desert Bloom Café, sweat was pooling in places I didn't even know *had* places.

Summer had barged in like an overzealous intern who'd mainlined six Red Bulls, and I was already drafting my resignation from The Mojave Desert, Inc., Summer Division. I yanked down the sun visor, which—thanks to my petite stature (i.e.: genetically cursed to be eye-level with steering wheels)—mostly framed the sky like a tragic art exhibit titled

"The Sun: Yes, It's Still There."

"Fuuuucking visor," I hissed, sitting on the tiptoe of my ass like a meerkat with a caffeine deficiency. *Please, Felicia,* I mentally pleaded, *have my coffee ready. Make it cold enough to freeze hell.*

By the time I parked, my cleavage had evolved into a microclimate. A greenhouse under each *globe*.

(Note: Buy stock in baby powder.)

I lunged for the café door, yelping as the handle seared my palm like a forgotten panini press. "Jesus H. Christ!" I yelped, briefly considering suing the sun for emotional damages.

Inside, the AC hit me like the Antarctic ice wall. I gasped, *alive again.*

"There you are," Felicia said, sliding over my cortado. "I added extra ice. You look like you wrestled a greased otter in a slip-'n-slide factory."

I grabbed the cup, downing it like a parched camel, wishing it was a Big Gulp instead. The caffeine hit my bloodstream like a motivational speaker on a sugar rush. *I am alive! I am powerful! I am… still sweating through my bra.*

I slumped into my usual seat, where the AC vent blew directly onto my forehead. Outside, the newly planted trees swayed smugly, sipping iced tea and laughing at my plight. "Show-offs," I muttered. But secretly, I admired their audacity. If a tree could thrive in Satan's armpit (i.e.: Vegas), maybe I could too. Or at least survive without being mistaken for a melted popsicle.

The heat had me daydreaming about truly rational life choices. Moving to Antarctica. Marinating in a kiddie pool of aloe vera. Trading my scrubs for a Yeti™-brand snowsuit. But then I remembered—I had a shower at home I planned to convert into a polar expedition. Arctic tundra vibes, here I come.

"How much longer?" I whined to Felicia, who looked about as ready to go as at the start of her shift.

"Ten minutes," she said, swatting the already clean counter with a rag. "Unless you want to power-wash me with the espresso machine."

"I would," I sighed, "but Shane would be mad, probably."

My thoughts inevitably drifted to Eric Mann—the tall, dark, and infuriatingly handsome UFC fighter who gymmed two doors down and had turned my life into a rom-com meets action movie. There was something about him—like a human electromagnet in a leather jacket, pulling me into his orbit with the subtlety of a fireworks show.

It wasn't exactly a secret that I often played Felicia's

Uber. Eric seemed to know it too. More than once, I'd caught him "casually" strolling toward the café just as I pulled up. Coincidence? Stalking? A secret side hustle as a parking lot influencer? I didn't ask questions.

After a parade of women had thrown themselves at him —including my ex-bestie, who stole my high school sweetheart like she was snatching the last pizza at a bridal shower—I'd finally let go of my crush. Our connection had mellowed into something friendlier, less "will they, won't they" and more "oh, hey, you're here again."

Still, I hadn't seen him in person since his first big fight— a night I attended in VIP, thank you very much—where I learned two things: 1) Blood is way louder in real life, and 2) Leather seats are a sweaty choice in May.

Instead, he'd slid into my DMs.

Of course, the fallout wasn't just about Eric. Everyone had seen my mortifying interview with Cheryl Marsh, the sports reporter who'd grilled me like I was the star of *Making a Murderer: UFC Edition*. I'd fallen for gossip again without fact-checking. *Dope!*

(Note: My life is basically a "What Not to Do" TikTok series sponsored by Regret™.)

Now, my name was trending again on social media— because why let a girl live in peace?—while Eric Mann was skyrocketing to fame like a rocket fueled by biceps and charisma. He'd been featured on podcasts, asked about those viral clips (you know, the ones where I accidentally became the internet's favorite hot mess), and somehow, I'd become the accidental muse to his rise. Think Shakespeare's muse, if Shakespeare's muse had tripped into a UFC ring.

I'd scrolled past meme after meme of The Misunderstanding: Fight Night Edition. There I was, forever frozen in pixelated shame "Eva's Guide to Viral Fame: Step 1) Yell at a Fighter. Step 2) Gossip?" Embarrassing? Sure. But at this point, my face was basically the poster child for "Oops, My Bad" moments. I'd leaned into the cringe like it was a yoga pose. *Namaste, humiliation, release.*

Eric, though? He had this way of talking about those embarrassing moments—so soft, so gentle—that it somehow made the humiliation sting less. I'd listened to him on a few podcasts, stunned by how candid he was about that unfortunate journey. He thought kinder about me than I did of myself sometimes.

Maybe that's why my stomach did a full Olympic floor routine when his DM popped up post-fight. Backflips! Cartwheels! A perfect 10 from the Russian judge!

At first, he explained he'd be MIA from the café scene for a few weeks—he needed to heal and rest.

(Translation: "I got punched in the face 87 times, but let's call it 'self-care.'")

I didn't blame him. If I'd won a fight that looked like a blender set to "puree," I'd need a vacation too. But for Eric, a "vacation" meant nonstop promo shoots, sponsorships, and grinning through interviews like his jaw wasn't held together by duct tape and prayer.

Strange as it was, that fight stirred up feelings I'd buried under a mountain of denial and Target clearance-rack wine. I'd never felt so fiercely protective of someone I'd publicly roasted like a holiday turkey. But I kept my distance. I hadn't confessed a thing—would I ever? The way I'd treated him had torched any chance of a rom-com ending. Now, we were just friends—a safe, uncomplicated label that let me sip my cortados without diving into the café's potted ferns every time he walked in.

Felicia slammed the espresso machine shut. "I'm almost done. Shane's nearly here."

"The same Shane who showed up an hour late to Brody's meltdown?" The guy was late more often than not, but at least he made good coffee.

"That's the one. If he ever opens a café, I'm naming my firstborn after him. Late-a-Latte."

Once Shane finally stumbled in, looking like he'd

wrestled a tumbleweed, we fled into the Vegas heat—a dry, oppressive monster that hugged you like a jealous ex—and braved the heat home. The drive had been fast, but brutal—like an episode of *Survivor, The Highlight Reel*.

Fanning herself with a napkin, Felicia started. "Have you heard about Tegan?"

I nearly tripped over my own resentment while slipping out of my too-hot Crocs. "Ugh. What now? Did she patent Photoshop Wedding, Inc.? Spot her at Gold Diggers Anonymous? Scott finally kick the bucket?"

Felicia rolled her eyes, slumping on the couch, her face tomato-red. "Worse. She's in hiding."

"Who cares!" I croaked. "It's her own doing. She's alienated herself, so *who freaking cares*."

Felicia leaning in, doing one of her "I found something I shouldn't've." "Well, yeah, but I did a *casual* Google search—"

"Casual?" I interrupted. "Felicia, your 'casual' searches could uncover Area 51's Wi-Fi password."

She ignored me, continuing, "—and stumbled onto a Subreddit called 'Where's Tegan?' It's part true crime, part 'where is this influencer?' type thing."

I gave in with a dramatic sigh and plopped down beside

her, letting the AC cool me down. "Well… is she… dead?"

"Jesus, Eva! She's just missing. *Allegedly.* The thread's got theories—you have to see it for yourself. It's mostly, 'Is she in hiding? Did she fake her death? Or—"

I cut her off again."—did she finally get canceled for that photoshopped wedding where her waist was smaller than her emotional IQ?"

"Eva! This is serious!"

"Alright, alright!"

"Another theory thrown around is that she's missing."

I scoffed. "As in *Gone Girl* missing or—"

She leaned in, tone more serious than my yearly pap. "As in 'Has Scott done *something* to her?' The thread's got receipts longer than the Food Network. Remember her 'cheap' wedding? Turns out the unedited photos Lexi sent us —the ones where the flowers looked like they'd been bought at a gas station—leaked. Now the internet's dragging her like a prom dress on a gravel road."

I winced, not buying it. "Okay, but Tegan thrives on drama. She'll spin this into a 'vulnerability journey' and sell scented candles called 'Resilience' by next week."

"Normally, I'd agree," Felicia said, lowering her voice like she was about to reveal the secret ingredient in Coca-

Cola. "But there's a video of her and Scott screaming at each other at Eric's fight. And now… radio silence? The Subreddit thinks she's…"

"Dead?" I whispered, half-wishing (*oh, come on*), half-intrigued.

"Eva!" Felicia groaned. "Can you take this seriously?"

I blinked. "How sure are you she's not just on a second—or, let's be honest, a *real*—honeymoon?"

She shook her head, stubborn as a burro in the desert. "Someone would've spotted her already. Linked an IP address to a post or something. She's MIA, Eva."

I slumped back, trying to process. Tegan had everything —a trust fund, a mansion, a husband who probably had a pulse. Why vanish?

"Unless…" I gasped, a wild theory forming. "What if she is pulling a *Gone Girl*?"

"Why would she—"

"Yes! Fake her own disappearance to reboot her brand! It's genius. Disturbing, but genius." I snapped my fingers, the idea taking root. "Or," I countered, "she finally realized no amount of Photoshop can fix Scott's personality and she's better off… disappearing?"

Felicia shook her head, her curls bouncing.

"What is it, then?"

"That's the bad part. The Subreddit thread thinks Tegan's *missing* missing."

CHAPTER

TWO

THE RECEPTION AREA WAS quieter than a library during a nap strike—which, of course, meant the lobby at Boring Nondescript Medical was heaving with patients. It was one of those days where the universe clearly thought, "Let's see how many minor crises we can cram into 24 hours!" I shuffled to the front desk, already mentally drafting my resignation letter in Comic Sans. Morgan—Claire's so-called "temporary" replacement—had called in sick *again*. At this rate, I was convinced she was either a figment of our collective imagination or the victim of a voodoo curse.

The doctors' wives were *supposed* to rotate in during emergencies, per the sacred "Spousal Duty Clause" (a.k.a., the unspoken pact scribbled on a napkin late 2020). But let's be real: their commitment level rivaled a cat's interest in fetch. They'd vanish faster than free doughnuts at a gym, leaving the rest of us to play Tetris with patient appointments. And on days like today, the wouldn't even show up.

I checked in a frazzled mom, a guy with a suspiciously vibrant rash, and a toddler who'd swallowed a LEGO (parenting achievement unlocked?), then fled to the back office—my emotional bomb shelter.

Lexi stormed in moments later, her entrance rivaling a hurricane. "Why does the front desk look like the *Titanic* after the iceberg?" she demanded, slamming her bag down like it was Morgan.

"Morgan called off," I said, gesturing to the chaos beyond the door. "Again."

Lexi groaned, already unhappy. "She's either faking the flu or starring in a COVID, The Resurgence episode. Check the schedule—it's Jacinda's turn today."

I sighed, resigned. Jacinda, the human embodiment of "fashionably late." She'd glide in at noon, trailing organic kale dust and a story about "traffic" (code for: "My alarm didn't go off."). We'd all pretend not to notice, because confronting her would require energy we'd earmarked for surviving the day.

Desperate to derail the doom spiral, I blurted, "What's

this about Tegan going AWOL?"

Lexi froze, her gossip radar pinging like a metal detector at a beach. "Tegan? Missing?" She leaned in, her tone shifting to TMZ correspondent. "Since when?"

The question hung in the air, thick as the clinic's hand sanitizer. Asking about Tegan wasn't just gossip—it was emotional archaeology. Digging up the ghost of friendships past, the one who'd left my life looking like a post-riot crime scene. Some wounds never heal; they just scab over and itch at inconvenient times.

"Since Felicia told me yesterday."

She shrugged. "Charles hasn't mentioned it, and Scott's been weirdly quiet. But you know Tegan—she's probably off planning her second honeymoon—outside her house this time."

"That's what I told Felicia, but she's insistent."

"Maybe she's finally been arrested for crimes against monogamy," Lexi mused, tapping her nails on the desk. "Wouldn't put it past her."

I forced a laugh, but the bitterness lingered, sharp as a paper cut.

No one had heard a peep about Tegan since Eric's fight night—not even Lexi, had spilled a crumb about her boyfriend's best friend's wife. Normally, I'd be drowning in Tegan Updates™ by now—"She's divorcing Scott! She's joining a cult! She's trademarked her eyelash curler!"—but radio silence. Lexi was tighter-lipped than a CIA operative at a family reunion.

I'd half-expected her to be juggling her two boyfriends like a circus act—Charles, the silver-fox TFMAM (Trust Fund Middle-Aged Man), and Brody, the walking protein shake—but nope. Lexi's lips were sealed, and it was infuriating.

"Felicia said the Subreddit think Tegan's either missing or in hiding."

Lexi's eyes narrowed into emerald laser beams. "So Felicia's source is that *super credible* Subreddit where conspiracy theorists argue about Bigfoot's skincare routine?"

"It is a credible forum," I lied. "They've got screenshots. Flowcharts. A mood board."

Lexi snorted. "Eva, Tegan isn't 'missing.' She's lying low because someone leaked her real wedding photos with all the bad decor, and she looked less 'Instagram goddess' and more 'sleep-deprived raccoon.' She posted a heavily filtered selfie this morning with a caption about 'self-care journeys.' She's fine."

"But Felicia said—"

"Felicia doesn't know anything about anything. And she thinks Scott's involved?" Lexi cut in. "Oh, please. Next you'll tell me he's hiding her in a bunker with Elvis and the Loch Ness Monster."

"She used to post three times a day! Now it's radio silence!"

"Not silence—*strategy*," Lexi said, waving a hand like she was swatting a fly. "She's rebranding. From 'Bridezilla' to 'Victim of the Patriarchy.'"

I squinted at her. "You were at her wedding. You sent us those candid photos."

"Coincidence," Lexi said breezily. "And no, I didn't leak them. But whoever did is a national hero."

"Lexi—"

"Eva, you hate Tegan," she snapped, leaning in. "Why the sudden Nancy Drew act? You're not jealous she's finally irrelevant, are you?"

"No, I couldn't care less." The words hung in the air, sharp as a guillotine. Jealous? Of Tegan? *Please*.

"Make up your mind," Lexi said, tossing her dark hair extensions. "You can't despise her and play Concerned Citizen of the Year. Pick a lane, Eva. Preferably one that doesn't involve me driving to Tegan's McMansion in this heat."

I shrugged, my expression a masterpiece of conflicting emotions. "I don't like her, but I don't want her kidnapped by aliens either."

(Translation: I'd rather she haunt my life than my conscience.)

Lexi sighed, her frustration visible. "She's not missing! She's just avoiding the internet because her wedding photos made her look like she got married in a dumpster. But fine— let's go stalk her. Maybe she'll insult your outfit, you'll remember why you hate her, and we can all go home before Felicia starts a GoFundMe for 'Tegan's Underground Bunker.'"

I groaned. Confronting Tegan was about as appealing as a root canal, but Lexi had a point—Felicia's theories were spiraling faster than a TikTok conspiracy thread. "Fine. But if she mentions my hair, I'm blaming you."

"Deal," Lexi said, grinning like she'd already won.

Later, I scooped up Felicia outside the café, where she stood clutching her iced cortado like it was the Holy Grail. The heat was brutal, the air felt like a Silvia Plath—*never mind*—but Felicia looked annoyingly unfazed, as if she'd been genetically engineered in a lab labeled "Desert Dweller."

"Why are you outside?" I hissed, blasting the AC like I was trying to freeze time itself. "It's 110 degrees! Are you part lizard?"

Felicia slid into the passenger seat, zero heat damage. "Shane was actually on time today. And I found out something juicy."

"If it's another Subreddit theory about Tegan joining a cult—"

"Better," she interrupted, her eyes gleaming.

"I'm still… processing," Felicia said, her voice wobbling like a Jenga tower in an earthquake. She was practically vibrating with suppressed drama, and I was this close to shaking her like a soda can.

"What did you find," I demanded, already growing tired of her guessing game.

Felicia's eyes darted around like she was being surveilled by the FBI. Then, with the gravitas of someone announcing a royal scandal, she hissed, "Tegan has a sex tape."

I choked on my coffee so hard I'm pretty sure I coughed up a lung. "What?"

"That's what the Subreddit says!" Felicia whisper-yelled, as if Tegan was within earshot.

"The Subreddit also thinks Bigfoot runs a gluten-free bakery in Oregon!" I shot back, wiping coffee off my chin. "Lexi says Tegan's fine. She posted a video today blaming her photoshopping on 'bad lighting' and 'haters with no boundaries.'"

Felicia's face scrunched up like I'd just insulted her sourdough starter. "Oh, please. Lexi's probably in on it. She's Tegan's unofficial publicist! She knew about the pegging thing before anyone!"

"First of all, *no one* needed to know about the pegging thing," I muttered, shuddering at the memory. "Second, she gets Tegan tea because of Charles, you know that. It's not like she goes digging for it like an unpaid FBI agent. Third, a sex tape? Lexi would've sold tickets to that circus by now."

"Maybe she's saving it for a rainy day!" Felicia countered, her voice rising. "Or—*or*—maybe Tegan's hiding it to protect Scott's 'legacy' or whatever."

My brain short-circuited. Tegan? A sex tape? Scott Van Hoff, erotic asphyxiation enthusiast and pegging connoisseur? This was less *Real Housewives* and more *Black*

Mirror—first episode *Black Mirror? Shudder.*

"This is insane," I said, clutching the wheel like a stress ball. "Even for Tegan."

"Insane?" Felicia leaned in, her eyes glittering with mischief. "Or brilliant? Think about it—Tegan's a master at rebranding. From 'Bridezilla' to 'Victim of the Patriarchy' to… *adult film pioneer*? She's unstoppable."

I buried my face in my hands. "I need a vacation. Or a lobotomy."

"Too late," Felicia said, tilting her phone screen my way. The Subreddit thread glowed ominously. "The people have spoken. And the people want answers."

Once home, I slumped on the kitchen counter, glad to see the sink empty. *Thank you, Felicia.*

"It's not *confirmed* confirmed," Felicia said, leaning against the countertop with the gravitas of a spy revealing nuclear codes, "only because Deeznuts2001 hasn't dropped the link yet. But the thread's on fire. Everyone thinks it's legit."

I snorted, nearly inhaling my iced coffee. "Deeznuts2001? Felicia, that username alone screams 'trustworthy source.' Next you'll tell me the Pentagon's leaking secrets via TikTok dances."

"Don't laugh!" she hissed, though her lips twitched. "This is serious! Why else would Tegan vanish? She's been MIA since that night at Eric's fight—when she and Scott were screaming louder than the referee!"

"Oh, I remember," I said, the mental image flashing like a cringe-worthy meme. "She was yanking Scott's arm so hard I thought she'd dislocate it. But, still."

"Exactly," Felicia said, jabbing her straw at me for emphasis. "And guess who was ringside, livestreaming the whole meltdown? *Deeznuts2001*. They've got receipts. Screenshots. A timeline."

"Holy fuck," I breathed, the pieces crashing together like a toddler's Lego tower. "So Tegan's sex tape scandal is… crowdsourced?"

Felicia's eyes gleamed like she'd just won the lottery. "And *I'm* trending in the thread now! I commented, 'Ask me anything,' and they figured out I was the barista from the viral video! I've got, like, followers."

I gaped at her. "You're telling me you're Subreddit-famous because of that viral video?" *The one where I'd erroneously called Eric a "disgusting pig." Ugh.*

"Yup," she said, flipping her hair with faux modesty. "I'm basically an influencer now. *Deeznuts2001* DM'd me a popcorn emoji. It's chaos."

"Chaos? You're the Homer Simpson vanishing into the hedge meme of this drama!"

"Hey," she said, grinning like a Cheshire cat, "I don't make the rules. I just ride the dumpster fire."

"So, let me get this straight," I said. "You joined a conspiracy Subreddit about Tegan's *alleged* sex tape using your real name?"

Felicia fiddled with her nail polish, suddenly very interested in a chip. "Not exactly."

I shot her a look sharper than a sushi chef's knife.

"Fine," she huffed, like I'd just asked her to donate a kidney. "It's *FeliciaMooreCakes*. But it's subtle!"

I gaped at her. "Subtle? That's like writing 'Secret Spy' on your forehead in glitter glue!"

She waved a hand, dismissing me. "They're lovely people! And when I mentioned I know you and Eric IRL? Chaos. You're basically their Taylor Swift. They've got theories about your hair, your scrubs, that time you tripped over a fire hydrant—"

"Wait, what?" I squeaked, my pulse quickening. "What else do they know? Do they have my third-grade report card?

My Netflix queue?"

"Relax. It's mostly harmless," Felicia chirped, scrolling through her phone like it held the secrets of the universe. "The Subreddit sleuths have pieced together your entire life from that viral video. Your job, the café, Eric's gym… They've probably got a mood board of your daily routine. But here's the kicker—they also know Tegan stole your high school boyfriend *and* that you're my personal Uber driver. None of that was in the video! These people are like truffle pigs for drama."

I stared at her, my coffee halfway to my mouth. "What the hell? Are they FBI agents? Or just bored stalkers with Wi-Fi?"

Felicia shrugged, unfazed. "They're thorough. If they say Tegan's gone full *Gone Girl* and has a sex tape, I'm buying popcorn and tuning in."

"Holy crap," I muttered, a chill skittering down my spine. I swatted the panic away. No way was I letting Reddit's basement-dwelling keyboard warriors live rent-free in my head.

"Tegan's fine," I insisted. "She posted a video today looking smugger than a cat who stole cream."

"Oh, Eva," Felicia sighed, patting my arm like I'd just admitted I believed in the Tooth Fairy. "You think filtered sunlight and a hashtag prove she's alive? Please."

"Want to play detective with us, then?" I said, dangling the bait. "Lexi's plotting a stakeout at Tegan's McMansion. We'll wear disguises. Sunglasses. Maybe fake mustaches."

Felicia's eyes lit up, then dimmed. "Can't. Shane's 'managing' the café, which means I'll be single-handedly averting the apocalypse. Again."

I huffed. "Fine. But if I survive this recon mission, you have to drop the sex tape theory. Swear on your sourdough starter."

Felicia's grin stretched wider than a yoga influencer's leggings. "Deal. But if Tegan's got a secret dungeon, I want exclusive rights to the thread."

CHAPTER

THREE

"THIS IS *PATHETIC*," I grumbled, shielding my eyes from the Vegas glare like the sun had a personal vendetta against my melatonin levels. While Lexi strutted ahead in her gold digger uniform—morning glow intact—I waddled behind in my dupe Lululemon leggings, each squeaky step a humiliating reminder that my life choices had officially hit rock bottom.

Felicia's Reddit rabbit hole had morphed into a full-blown true-crime circus. Per the keyboard warriors of *r/JusticeForRichPeople*, Tegan Van Hoff had ghosted the planet after a screaming match with her husband, Scott "Totally-Not-A-Sociopath (Promise)" Van Hoff. The whole mess reeked of a Bravo special guest-starring a subpoena, but Lexi—queen of catastrophes—had declared us "investigative journalists."

"Steps. We're here for steps," I muttered, my Fitbit vibrating like a chastity belt as we speed-walked past a coven of TFMAMs (Trust Fund Middle-Aged Moneybags™) clinking mimosas at dawn. The Wynn's lobby was a dystopian mashup of frozen Botox grins and Birkins older than my student loans—a nursing home for people who think "quiet luxury" means screaming their net worth.

"Switch," Lexi barked, thudding her Chanel at my chest.

"*Why?*"

"Because we look like FBI interns who raided a Ross Dress-for-Less," she snapped, prying my bag from my grip like it was radioactive. "This is Vegas, Eva. Pretend you've heard of Amex."

"It's not Ross," I complained. "It's Nordstrom Rack," I hissed, clutching my purse like it owed me rent. "That's basically designer!"

Lexi's gasp could've sucked the collagen out of the room. "Oh, honeybee. No." With the finesse of a Vegas magician, she dumped my tampons and half-eaten Clif Bar into her quilted Chanel and pitched mine into a trash can. It landed with a thud, as dignified as my dating history.

"Lexi!" I lunged, but she yanked me forward, arm looped through mine like she was wrangling a feral Chihuahua.

"Relax, it's an upgrade," she purred. "Smile like you're flirting with a prenup. My mom's old stripper trick. The bigger the smile, the bigger the tip. Works on everyone except the IRS."

"We're not here to scam retired hairlines," I muttered, nostalgic for Felicia's café chaos—where the pinnacle of danger was Shane "accidentally" putting almond milk in my oat milk cortado.

"Please," Lexi scoffed, eyeing a chandelier like she was calculating its pawn value. "These people drop more on brunch than your car's worth. You need a trust fund just to breathe the air-conditioning here."

"We're breathing the AC here," I muttered, perching on a lounge chair like a seagull at a sushi bar.

"Exactly," Lexi said, flicking her hair with the elegance of a Kardashian dodging paparazzi.

We'd hijacked a poolside table, blending in as gracefully as duct tape on a Chanel handbag. My leg jittered under the table—*why are we chasing Tegan?* The woman was insufferable. Then my phone vibrated.

A grin betrayed me.

"Spill the tea or I spill your drink," Lexi hissed, leaning in like a TMZ reporter.

"Air," I lied, cheeks burning like a sidewalk in Death Valley. "Just… air."

But it wasn't air. It was Eric—UFC's answer to a Nicholas Sparks cover model—bombarding my DMs since his fight night. Apologies for the UFC exploiting our viral video (corporate jargon for *cash grab*), gratitude for my "support" (translation: me screeching "Stop bleeding!" when he went down in the ring), and enough heart-eyes emojis to give a nun hives. It felt like starring in a Netflix rom-com… if the meet-cute involved stalking his wannabe ex through a casino.

Keeping Eric in the friend zone wasn't just about Tegan—our human grenade of a mutual ex (ex friend and ex stalker, that is!)—or the fact our history dangled between us like a buffering Netflix screen. It was the tiny panic gremlin in my skull shrieking, "He'll throw himself outta your life—again!" But with every "Still owe you that coffee" text, the gremlin's voice faded, replaced by my dumb heart doing parkour.

His latest DM lit up my screen.

Eric: Missing your scowls at the café. Coffee when I'm back?

Miss. A word that hit like a THC margarita—smooth, buzzy, and 100% trouble.

"What's Thor's hotter cousin want now?" Lexi muttered, elbow-jabbing me as a baby-faced server shuffled over, eyeing us like we'd smuggled in a raccoon.

"I don't... recognize you?" he stammered, clutching his tablet like a security blanket.

Lexi swiveled with the lethal grace of a reality TV villain, smile sharp enough to fillet sushi. "Sweetheart," she crooned, flipping her hair with the drama of a Pantene commercial, "fetch me a French 75. Dom Pérignon. And my tragically single friend—" she jerked a stiletto-nailed thumb at me, "—needs an Aperol spritz. Snappy."

The kid blinked, sweat glistening like a Vegas slot machine. "But... who's paying?"

I nervous giggled, but Lexi leaned in, her vanilla aura smothering him like a designer weighted blanket. "Room 3402. Mrs. Van Hoff."

He paled. "Mrs. Van Hoff is—"

"Parched," Lexi cut in, widening her eyes to cult-leader levels of intensity. Her smile stayed sweet, but her tone could've iced a wedding cake. "Scott's new wife. So scurry, cupcake. And if you mention this to anyone, I'll donate your tips to his alimony fund."

The server blanched, his name tag ("Hi, I'm Trevor!")

practically trembling. "But… Mrs. Van Hoff is blonde," he squeaked, clutching his tray like a life raft.

Lexi arched a brow, her smirk widening. "I dyed it. *And* my patience. Care to test which one fades faster?"

He fled.

"Jesus," I muttered, watching him nearly trip over a potted palm. "You practically made him cry."

Lexi inspected her nails, serene as a monk. "Please, I was charming. He'll thank me later.. Confidence is a public service."

"More like a war crime," I mumbled, sinking lower in my chair. The guilt was already gnawing at me, but this was classic Lexi—dragging me into morally gray areas like they were sample sales.

She leaned back, sunglasses sliding down her nose as she fixed me with a look. "Life hack, Eva: Walk into any room like you're the CEO of everything. Fake it till you bankrupt it."

For a split second, I almost believed her. Then I remembered what she'd done for her brand new Porsche ("Oh, come on! Just toes!").

"Or," I said, eyeing Trevor as he whisper-screamed into a walkie-talkie, "we could *not* commit felonies before lunch?"

Lexi waved a hand, already scrolling her phone. "Relax. By tomorrow, Trevor'll be bragging he survived a conversation with me. He'll be fine."

I straightened my spine, channeling Lexi's unshakable vibe. *Own the room. Own the casino. Own the potted fern if you have to.* Lexi's confidence wasn't just confidence—it was a superpower, polished to a lethal shine by what I called her "supermodel sorcery." Men tripped over themselves to fetch her drinks; waiters genuflected. It was equal parts inspiring and terrifying.

As we sipped our ill-gotten cocktails, the conversation drifted like a wayward Uber driver.

"Still no ring?" I asked, already knowing the answer. Lexi's left hand was as bare as a Kardashian's conscience.

"Nope," she said, swirling her champagne. "I'll marry the fossil when he ditches the prenup. A girl's got standards."

I raised a brow. "Even after your *medicate-and-litigate* masterplan?"

She smirked. "Trust me, I thought about it. But no, I'd rather not litigate at all—unless I drug him into submission."

I choked on my spritz. "That's… almost ethical of you."

"Please," Lexi scoffed. "Charles isn't some blushing virgin. He invented shady deals. Besides, after I flaunted

Brody at Eric's fight? VIP section, legs for days? I thought he'd drop to one knee just to spite Brody's abs."

I snorted. Brody was distractingly hot, if a little dangerous—like a Greek god with anger issues. "Or maybe Charles is immune to your Jedi mind tricks. He's a TFMAM, Lex. They're born with a sixth sense for gold diggers."

"Damn, Eva. Since when did you turn into Warren Buffett?" Lexi smirked, swirling her champagne like it was a crystal ball of judgment.

I grinned, basking in the rare glow of outsmarting her. "Since I realized your 'TFMAM Chronicles' are just Rich People Problems: The Audiobook. Now spill—what's the deal with Brody?"

Lexi leaned back, her smirk sharpening. "Brody's a human scratch-off ticket. Fun to play with, but you don't cash him in. Sure, he's got the face of a Disney prince and the body of a Marvel extra, but his life plan? 'Win fights, buy protein powder.' Tragically uncertain."

I snorted. "So you're saying he's all biceps, no 401(k)?"

"Exactly," she said, pointing her straw at me. "He's a golden retriever in a Gucci belt. Adorable, but if you ask him to solve a math problem, he'd whimper. I need a man who can quote *The Art of War*, not just bench-press it."

"Sounds like you're into him way more than you're admitting," I teased, dodging her napkin toss.

"Please," Lexi scoffed. "I need a man who can fund my lifestyle *and* my lawsuits. Brody's idea of 'investing' is buying two Monster Energy drinks at once."

"So you want… a CEO who moonlights as your personal philanthropist?"

"Yes. I need more than a pretty fuckboy." She paused, eyes narrowing. "Which reminds me—don't think I didn't notice you blushing at Eric's DMs. You're over there giggling like a teen with a crush on a TikTok thirst trap."

I nearly choked on my spritz. "It's not Eric—"

"Liar," she sang, wagging a manicured finger. "You've got that 'he liked my selfie' glow."

Before I could retaliate, a flash of blonde streaked past. Tegan.

"Look," I whispered, ducking like we were in a spy thriller. "It's her!"

Lexi didn't even glance up. "See? She's not missing—she's rebranding. Her wedding video flopped harder than a soufflé in a hurricane. Now she's pivoting since her dumb video didn't hit."

"Why not?" I pressed, leaning in like a kid denied the last

cookie. Being blocked by Tegan was like getting kicked out of a group chat—petty, baffling, and weirdly motivating.

Lexi sipped her drink, her smirk sharp enough to slice through Tegan's ego. "Because aesthetics," she drawled, air-quoting with her manicured fingers, "are her entire personality. And when your 'luxury mansion' is just a Photoshop preset and prayer? People notice. Her influencer 'besties' are dropping her faster than a toxic TikTok trend. No one wants their brand tainted by her delulu."

I blinked. "So she's getting canceled for bad Photoshop?"

"Canceled? Honey, she's getting dragged. It's a full-on digital witch hunt. Even her collabs ghosted her. Turns out, nobody wants to promote a liar who edits her pool size."

Before I could savor the schadenfreude, a voice cut through the air.

"Brunette?" Tegan drawled, appearing behind us like a specter at a garden party. "As if I'd stoop to chestnut. I'm *platinum*, darling. Now, why's there a French 75 on my tab? I drink skinny margaritas, you sad Target regular."

Lexi didn't blink. "Call it a 'welcome back' gift," she said, toasting her with a smirk. "We were checking you weren't chained in a cheap wine cellar. Allegedly."

I piped up. "You're trending like a Ross sale. They think

Scott's buried you under his man cave."

Tegan's filler stayed frozen, but her left eyelid spasmed—a telltale flicker. "Missing?" She laughed, a sound like a champagne flute shattering. "I've been curating my absence. Building brand aura. Concepts you'd grasp if you'd ever left Vegas."

Lexi reclined, cool as a cucumber sandwich. "Brand aura? Or a breakdown? Your wedding photos had more Photoshop than a Snapchat puppy. Even your bouquet looked nicked from a funeral display."

Tegan's veneer wobbled. "I'm living the dream," she snapped, gesturing to the Wynn's lobby like it was Versailles. "Something you'll never sniff with your TJ Maxx energy."

"Tell that to your Reddit detectives," I shot back, "they're dissecting your life like a *Bake Off* technical. 'Tegan Van Hoff: Anatomy of a Train Wreck.'"

Tegan's porcelain complexion flushed. "They're nobodies," she hissed, voice trembling.

Lexi, ever the piranha, moved in. "Then why the fake mansion pics, Tegan? Were the real ones too... middle-class?" She clutched imaginary pearls. "Wait—did Scott's trust fund dry up? Is that why your infinity pool looked drawn by a toddler?"

Tegan's face turned the exact puce of a spoiled salmon cube. "I don't answer to failed gold diggers," she spat at Lexi, then wheeled on me. "Or you, Eva. Remember how easily I stole your sad little high school boyfriend? What was his name—Kyle? Kevin?" She snapped her fingers. "Like taking Haribo from a toddler."

I grinned, slow and glacial. "Aww, Tegan. Still clinging to the past? Meanwhile, Eric Mann—champion, heartthrob, human Adonis—is sliding into my DMs like a TikTok thirst trap. Denied you publicly, didn't he? *Oops*. Publicly chose me over you, didn't he? *Awks*."

Lexi snorted loud enough to startle a nearby waiter into dropping a tray of caviar bites. "Eric Fucking Mann vs. Scott Van Snooze? Brutal."

Tegan's Botox quivered under the assault. "Go to hell."

"Already there, babe," I chirped, waving as she stormed off, heels clacking like a metronome of fury.

Lexi raised her glass. "To Eva—finally weaponizing her *Bridget Jones* era."

I exhaled, feeling lighter despite the tension. Years of Tegan's barbed comments dissolved quicker than an Alka-Seltzer in Prosecco.

Take notes, Taylor Swift.

CHAPTER

FOUR

IT WAS ANOTHER GIRLS' night—my holy grail. A sacred ritual of bottom shelf liquor, scandalous confessions, and laughter so violent it counted as core exercise. After surviving Tegan's latest verbal assassination attempt at the Wynn, I needed this like a drought needs rain—badly.

Cali's backyard was our unofficial HQ, a *Homes & Gardens*-worthy haven currently masquerading as Satan's sun lounger. The Vegas heat clung to us like a staticky onesie, but her pool glimmered temptingly, even if it threatened to morph my blowout into a frizz bomb. *Priorities, Eva. Sanity over style. Probably.*

"Ta-da!" Cali announced, waddling over with a tray of margaritas, her bump leading the charge like a VIP. "And before you ask—no, I'm not 'overdoing it,'" she added, side-eyeing my concerned frown. "I'd rather melt into a puddle of maternity leggings than miss Felicia's recap of Shane's latest caramel macchiato disaster. The man could burn water."

I patted her stomach, half-expecting a tiny fist to emerge demanding a Costco membership. "This child owes you years of spa days. You're gestating a human and hosting a made-for-TV episode for chaos."

"Please," Cali snorted. "This kid's already kicking to the beat of Felicia's rants. Pre-born for gossip."

The girls trickled in, armed with Trader Joe's snacks and gossip hotter than jalapeños. But the real showstopper was Claire—postpartum, glowing like Kate Middleton after a *Vogue* shoot, if Kate Middleton had ever rocked mascara smudges and a muslin cloth slung over one shoulder.

"Look at her," Felicia whispered, clutching her chest. "Motherhood's her superpower. She's like... Gwyneth Paltrow with a diaper bag."

"And yet she still laughs at your dad jones," I said, watching Claire settle into a lounge chair like it was a throne.

"So Marc says, 'Guess I'm a motherfucker now,'" Claire announced, dropping the punchline with a grin.

The group cackled—a sound 20% genuine amusement, 80% trauma-bond hysteria.

"At least he's self-aware," Cali said, sipping her virgin

piña colada with the solemnity of a sommelier. "My cousin's husband bought her a vacuum for their first anniversary. A vacuum. She filed for divorce by Valentine's Day."

Claire shrugged, unfazed as pool water splashed into her margarita. "I pushed a human out of my body. Marc's lucky I let him *speak*."

We clinked glasses, toasting to chaos, camaraderie, and the unspoken rule of girls' night: *What's said by the pool stays by the pool.*

"Amen!" Cali chimed, grinning like she'd just won a mom-of-the-year trophy (which, let's be honest, she had). "But enough about diapers and midnight feedings—what's the *tea*?"

Felicia leaned forward, eyes sparkling with the fervor of a true-crime podcaster. "So, apparently, Tegan's not missing—she's just hiding from her own Instagram filters. But get this: there's a Subreddit dedicated to her drama. They're calling it 'TeganGate.'"

Claire nearly dropped her margarita. "A Subreddit? Is that like a digital book club?"

"She's lying," Lexi said, splashing like a toddler mid-tantrum. "I looked for the thread and found nothing. *Zilch. Nada.*"

Felicia huffed. "Well, since I have higher than an 8th grade education, I did. And I found it in, like, two clicks. Lexi couldn't even Google her way out of a paper bag."

Lexi scoffed, flicking a cucumber slice off her plate. "Please. I found Tegan *in person* while you were busy deep-diving into conspiracy theories. Turns out, she's just allergic to cyberstalkers."

"Oh, sorry," Felicia shot back, "I forgot your detective skills peak at stalking exes through casino security cams."

I winced. "Girls!" Their bickering was like a tennis match where everyone loses.

"Anyway," Felicia plowed on, "the Subreddit's convinced there's a sex tape. *Allegedly*."

Lexi rolled her eyes so hard I worried they'd stick. "Everyone has a sex tape, Felicia. My dog probably has one. The real question is—who'd watch?—Scott? He'd fall asleep halfway through."

"So there *is* a sex tape?" Claire asked.

"Probably just rumors of a sex tape, if anything," Lexi said, throwing daggers at Felicia—with her eyes.

Felicia's eye twitched. "You're just scared they'll dig up your secrets next. What's your Reddit handle? GoldDiggerBarbie?"

"At least I'm not posting cappuccino art in a thread debating Tegan's hair extensions!" Lexi snapped, her voice rising.

Claire sipped her drink, unfazed. "Girls, this is better than my postpartum soap operas. Please continue."

"Enough!" Cali interjected, clinking her glass like a judge with a gavel. "Lexi, spill. Has Charles finally proposed? Or is he still clinging to that prenup like a toddler to a security blanket?"

Lexi's posture snapped from defensive to diva in milliseconds. "He bought me a new condo," she purred, tossing her hair. "But the prenup? Still tighter than his Botox."

I gasped. "You left the high-rise? The one with the chandelier that looked like it was stolen from Versailles?"

"Babe, chandeliers are so 2019," Lexi said, sipping her martini with the elegance of a Bond villain. "I upgrade homes like some people upgrade Wi-Fi. Charles insists. Says it's cheaper than therapy."

Felicia muttered, "Bet he's paying for both," under her breath, loud enough to make Claire snort margarita out her nose.

"What was that?" Lexi hissed, leaning in like a hawk

spotting a mouse. "Speak up, Felicia. Or did your barista budget finally cut out your vocal cords?"

Felicia met her glare, sweet as arsenic. "I said, 'Bless your heart.' You know—Southern for 'Go to hell.'"

Claire, ever the diplomat, jumped in. "I'd rather birth twins in a Walmart than move yearly. How do you do it?"

"Oh, I don't do anything," Lexi said, waving a hand adorned with a rock the size of a golf ball. "Charles hires movers. I supervise. Horizontally."

Felicia's eye twitched. "Must be exhausting, lying there like a starfish while other people pack your gold-plated flatware."

"Jealousy's a disease, Felicia," Lexi sighed. "Get well soon."

The air crackled with enough tension to power a Tesla. Cali, sensing catastrophe, lobbed a breadstick at Lexi's head. "Play nice, or I'll revoke your charcuterie privileges."

Lexi caught it mid-air, grinning. "Fine. But only because I want details on Claire's 'motherfucker' story. Did Marc at least get you a push present? Or just a participation trophy?"

"Lexi, he's broke," Claire said, biting into a cracker. "My push present was an extra week off work."

Lexi's eyes widened to the size of a charger plate. *"Oof."*

Felicia, unable to stay out of it, chirped in. "Listen to Lexi long enough and you'll learn how to suck the dollars out of his wallet."

"Babe, I'd never advise you," Lexi drawled. "Unless you want lessons on how to not dress like a toddler's finger-painting project." The poolside fell silent, save for the faint gurgle of Claire choking on her virgin mojito.

"At least I'm not auctioning myself off to geriatric sugar daddies!" Felicia shot back, flinging a cucumber slice for emphasis. It missed Lexi's head by an inch and splatted against a palm.

Classic Felicia—bad aim, worse timing.

"Girls!" I pleaded, waving my margarita like a white flag. "Can we not turn Cali's pool into *Jerry Springer: Aqua Edition*?"

Claire, ever the serene chaos-lover, shrugged. "I'm just here for the snacks. Carry on."

Lexi's composure wavered, revealing a crack in her Chanel armor. "My *boyfriend* spoils me rotten," she sniffed, "and my mother FaceTimes me daily. How's *yours*? Still framing your law school rejection letter?"

Felicia's eyes narrowed to laser precision. "My mom's not

the one charging by the hour at the Golden Years Lounge!"

The gasp was collective. Cali, mid-sip, spat her mocktail into the pool. "Okay, new rule: No mom-shaming unless it's my mother in-law. She still thinks quinoa is a Pokémon."

I waded into the pool, heels sinking into the mossy tiles like my dignity. "Ladies, please. You're scaring the guppies."

"You wish your mom taught you more than rejection!" Lexi lobbed back, splashing water with the ferocity of a disgruntled mermaid.

Felicia snorted. "And you wish yours taught you self-respect! Newsflash—Charles isn't your boyfriend. He's your *sponsor*."

Lexi lunged, but the pool turned her fury into a slow-motion pratfall. "I'm *exclusive* with Charles!" she hissed, mascara bleeding down her cheeks like a weepy raccoon.

"Exclusive?" Felicia barked. "So Brody's just your charity case? Or is he your 'fitness consultant'? Your mom must be proud," she said, nearly capsizing a floating tray of deli meats.

That was the final straw. Felicia had crossed a line—a line Lexi guarded more fiercely than her secret stash of designer sale receipts. Lexi's past wasn't just messy; it was a bomb of disaster—a childhood spent ducking her mother's dance routine (a pole routine that included a $5 steak and lobster meal downtown) and a rotating cast of "uncles" who lasted about as long as a 7-Eleven 2 for 1 deal.

So when Lexi launched herself at Felicia, it was less Elegant Avenger and more Tasmanian Devil in False Eyelashes. If not for Cali—waddling into the fray like a penguin piloting a hot air balloon—Lexi might've actually scalped her with a manicured nail. Felicia, belatedly realizing she'd prodded a honey badger in Louboutins, backpedaled so fast she tripped over a pool noodle and face-planted into a plate of guac.

Chaos, thy name was girls' night. Claire yowled, "Not the guac!" as the dip torpedoed into the deep end. I, meanwhile, morphed into a UN peacekeeper, hollering, "Ladies! This isn't *Jerry Springer*!" while steering Cali inside before her toddler could Instagram the carnage with a juice-stained iPad.

Lexi ricocheted around the pool, stiletto sandals sinking into turf like it was quicksand, screeching, "You're just jealous Charles bought me two condos!"

Felicia, now barricaded behind a palm tree, fired back, "Jealous? Honey, my self-respect's rent-controlled!"

Claire, ever the bard of despair, sniffled into a margarita glass, "This is worse than Marc gifting me a foot massager for our anniversary…"

The insults flew like rogue confetti at a bachelorette:

Lexi: "You couldn't afford the lint in my Birkin!"

Felicia: "At least my mom didn't teach me to monetize men!"

Lexi: "No, she just taught you to give it away for free!"

It fizzled out as abruptly as champagne left in the sun. Felicia, realizing she'd exhausted both comebacks and her bottom shelf tequila, fled with the grace of a meerkat evading a hawk. We spent the next hour fishing avocado chunks from the filter and pretending we hadn't just witnessed emotional arson.

"Next time," Cali groaned, scrubbing queso from her bump, "let's just… knit. Or join a nunnery. Or go into witness protection."

But beneath the rubble of ruined dip and shattered egos, the truth lingered: Lexi's Chanel armor hid deep discount-store scars, Felicia's barista hustle masked Ivy League ghosts and maternal rejection, and we were all just one bad day away from becoming our mothers.

CHAPTER

FIVE

PILATES WAS SUPPOSED TO be zen. Instead, it felt like a hostage negotiation with my own hamstrings. But after the girls' night that could've been titled Apocalypse Now: Poolside, I needed to sweat out my rage more than I needed oxygen. As I lunged and cursed and lunged again, I imagined each bead of sweat carrying away a tiny grievance: *That's for Felicia's passive-aggressive guac toss. This one's for Lexi criticizing Felicia's one-nighters.* By the time I collapsed into a puddle of nylon and regret, I felt lighter—or maybe I was just delirious from oxygen deprivation.

But alas, my zen was as fleeting as a free sample, but the bitterness lingered. I was furious at Lexi and Felicia for turning our sacred girls' night into a *WWE Smackdown!* (*UFC: Throwdown?*), but mostly I was furious at myself for not bringing popcorn. And poor Cali—*pregnant, hormonal*

Cali—reduced to tears because her "tribe" had the emotional intelligence of feral raccoons. She'd been dreaming of guacamole and gossip, not a front-row seat to *Real Housewives: Desert Edition*.

When I ducked into the café, Felicia slid an iced cortado and a lemon-poppyseed tart across the counter like a peace offering. "Truce?" she said, eyes wide with desperation.

I eyed the tart, though. It was a work of art—golden, glazed, and probably laced with serotonin. Felicia had been baking like a woman possessed since Guy (bless his clueless soul) put her in charge of the summer menu. Rumor had it her new "Stress Scones" could cure existential dread in two bites.

"I'm sorry," she blurted, shoving the plate closer. "Not just for the pool noodle incident. For… everything."

I took a bite. The tart was stupidly good—zesty, buttery, with a crunch that whispered, "You're better than this drama." Against my will, I felt 12% less murderous.

"You're lucky you bake like a fairy godmother," I muttered, licking crumbs off my thumb.

Felicia grinned, relief softening her edges. "I also added vodka to the lemon curd. Guy thinks it's 'artisanal.'"

15% less murderous.

"You did go full *Game of Thrones* on her," I said, nibbling the crust. "But tearing Lexi's mom apart? That's *low* low. Harsh."

Felicia winced. "I know. I've been replaying it in my head on a loop. It's my new mental screensaver."

"Cali's forgiven you," I offered. "But Lexi's gone full ghost, practically. Even her patients are getting concerned. Yesterday, Mrs. Jimenez asked if she'd been replaced by a Stepford wife."

Felicia groaned. "I'll send her a fruit basket. Edible arrangement? No—a spa day. With champagne."

"Unless you can afford $500 champagne, stick with a text," I said. "Maybe just... 'Sorry I compared your life choices to a dumpster fire. xoxo.'"

Felicia snorted, then sobered. "What if she blocks me? Or worse—subtweets me?"

"You really fucked it, Fel."

Lexi wore her mother's past like a vintage Chanel jacket —expensive, complicated, and never to be mocked by peasants. She didn't flaunt it, but she didn't hide it either. Those hard-knock lessons—how to sweet-talk a landlord, how to spot a fake Rolex, how to exit a yacht before the money went bust—were her secret weapons. But Felicia kept poking at it like a kid jabbing a dead jellyfish, and that made Lexi's jaw twitch.

"I'll deal with Lexi when I see her," Felicia declared, swiping her apron from permanent milk stains. "But first— Tegan. The Subreddit's onto something."

I groaned. "The Subreddit? It might as well be Conspiracy Book Club 101?"

Felicia's eyebrow arched. "Maybe. But they're not entirely delusional. Did you see Tegan's latest post? That 'mansion' backdrop? I've seen better green screens in *Scooby-Doo*."

"We literally in-person-stalked her all the way to the Wynn Villas," I reminded her. "She's not missing. She's just... hiding."

"Exactly!" Felicia said, snapping her fingers. "Which means she's hiding *something*. No one uses that many Valencia filters unless they're laundering something. Emotions. Money. Souls."

I sighed. Felicia's Tegan obsession had escalated from hobby to habit, like doomscrolling but with conspiracy mood boards. Meanwhile, Lexi's feud with Felicia had morphed into a passive-aggressive Cold War, complete with subtweets and strategically timed Instagram unfollows. "You're spiraling. Tegan's fine. Lexi's the one we need to worry about."

"Why?" Felicia's voice cracked. She paused, then whispered, "It's not about Lexi, okay? Lexi's... whatever. This is bigger. Tegan's in deep."

I squinted. "Define deep. Like, 'forgot to renew her Botox' deep? Or 'accidentally married a con artist' deep?"

"I mean she's in trouble. Shouldn't that matter? We have to help her."

Felicia leaned in, her expression so grave I half-expected her to hand me a blood oath. "Scott's getting sued. For fraud. His hedge fund funneled cash into some crypto-metaverse-ponzi scheme, and now it's all... evaporated. Like, Scrooge McDuck vault, but empty."

My espresso shot threatened a comeback tour. "Evaporated? As in, 'poof, there goes my third yacht' evaporated? That's not fraud—that's *Succession* meets *Tiger King*."

"Exactly," Felicia hissed, shoving her phone at me. "The Subreddit's been tracking it. But the links keep disappearing. Scott's PR team's scrubbing the web faster than a toddler with a Sharpie."

I scrolled, but the main thread was 404'd. "Gone," I said, tossing her phone back. "Like my interest in this story, Fel."

"Eva, come on," Felicia muttered. "The rumors are everywhere. People are saying Tegan's been selling off her designer bags to cover legal fees. Allegedly."

I blinked. "Oh hell, this is just another 'Reddit Detectives' thing, then. Last time they 'exposed' a celeb affair, it was just the nanny. They never get anything right."

"She's drowning," Felicia said, her voice dropping to horror-movie trailer levels. "And if Scott sinks, she's his human life raft. Financially. Maybe legally. Who even knows anymore?"

I groaned. "Felicia, this is Reddit. Not *The Economist*. For all we know, Scott's 'fraud' is him using expired coupons at Whole Foods."

"Or," Felicia countered, "it's the biggest scandal since Enron. Either way, I'm not dropping it until I know the truth."

"What do I care?" I said, throwing my hands up like a beleaguered sitcom mom. "Felicia, Tegan's made my life— *our* life—a *telenovela*. Even if this crypto mess is real, what are we supposed to do? Stage an intervention? Bake her a 'Sorry Your Husband's a Fraud' cake?"

Felicia's eyes softened, which only annoyed me more. "I don't know—maybe warn her? Give her a heads-up?

Something."

I laughed, the sound sharp and bitter. "Remember the last time we saw her? She looked at me like I was a gum stain on her Louboutins. Why do you even care? You barely noticed her existence six months ago."

Felicia's gaze hardened. "Yeah, she's a nightmare, but no one deserves to be blindsided. What if it were you?"

Her big, pleading eyes sparked a flare of anger in me. *Where was this energy when Lexi needed it?* "But it's not," I said, my voice steadier than I felt. "And I don't think Tegan's in trouble. She's probably sipping margaritas in Cabo, laughing at us for falling for Reddit fan fiction."

"And if she is in trouble?" Felicia pressed, her voice soft but insistent.

"Then she can figure it out herself," I snapped. "We're not her fairy godmothers."

The door chimed, slicing through the tension like a chainsaw through buttercream. "Eric," I said, my irritation evaporating faster than my willpower near a sample sale. There he stood, UFC champion and accidental heartthrob, looking like he'd just body-slammed a cologne commercial and won.

"Real 'girl solidarity' move," Felicia hissed, gesturing to

the "Girls Just Wanna Have Fun" pin on her apron like it was a legal affidavit. But *puh-lease*—since when did girl code require resisting a man who smelled like a cedar forest and bad decisions?

(Translation: Tegan was on her own.)

He was slightly bruised—his face a watercolor of purples and yellows from his last fight—but honestly, it just made him look like a Renaissance painting titled "Chiseled Chaos." Mindy trailed behind him, glowing like she'd mainlined highlighter. If she'd just survived a roundhouse kick to the ribs, she hid it better than I hide my secret Dorito stash.

"Hi," Eric said, sliding into the seat beside me with ease. "Mind if I join?"

"Only if you promise not to arm-bar me," I said, ignoring Felicia's death stare. Girl solidarity could wait.

"Eric! The usual?" Felicia barked, scribbling his order—cappuccino and a tart? (Guess he was off that protein diet)—on a napkin like it was the Magna Carta. With that, the Tegan Conspiracy Summit was adjourned, and Felicia vanished behind the counter, muttering about "hormones over honor."

Mindy, meanwhile, strutted to the bar, her confidence blaring like a car alarm. I tried not to gawk, but it was like ignoring a flamingo in a bar.

"It's good to see you," Eric said, his voice softer than butter on toast. His eyes did that thing—that I-remember-the-DM-you-sent-at-2-AM thing—and suddenly, my heart was doing the salsa. Again.

"You too!" I chirped, sounding like a startled parakeet. *Be cool, Eva.*

His finger brushed against mine, and this time, I didn't pull away. Progress.

"I listened to your podcast," I said, my heart in my throat despite my efforts at cool and collected.

"Yeah?" He leaned in, his lashes framing his eyes (still faintly bruised) like they'd been drawn by a swoony Victorian poet. "What'd you think?"

"Loved it," I said, cheeks warming.

He smirked. "Which part?"

"All of it," I said, and it was so breathy, it was almost a whisper.

His grin widened. "The part about…you?

"Yeah. That part too," I mumbled, my voice so quiet it might as well have been a text message.

"It was all true, you know," he said, his tone loaded.

"Fuck me," Mindy said, sitting down between us, her

gravelly voice taking me out of the moment. "The sexual tension between you two is so thick I could cut it with a knife. Get a room already!" She kept talking, saying something about how dumb we were, wasting time when we could be doing—*ahem*—other things, and I blushed, looking at Eric blush, too.

(Translation: UFC Adonis wasn't immune to *emotions*.)

"And don't even get me started on that interview you did, Eva—me with Eric? In his *dreams*," she added, saying something about not giving impromptu interviews. Lesson learned.

Eric just kept looking at me, his smile steady, like he'd practiced it in front of a mirror. And for the first time since we'd met, I let myself actually like him. Not the "oh-my-god-he's-so-hot" kind of like, but the "oh-god-he's-actually-kind-of-lovely" kind. Which, frankly, was way more dangerous.

"So, about Tegan," Felicia chimed in, her milk-stained apron standing in between a very intense Eric and me.

"Not this again," I groaned.

"Fine," Felicia said, holding up her hands like she was surrendering to the FBI. "But if something happens to her, that's on you."

"If something happens to her, it's on *her*," I shot back,

because I was done being the designated Tegan apologist. "Now, can we please have a nice brunch with Eric and Mindy and figure out how to get you back in Lexi's good graces? Because—newsflash—you're not winning any 'Best Friend of the Year' awards right now."

Underneath it all, though, there was this weird, fizzy feeling—like champagne bubbling in my chest. Regret, desire, and the faintest whisper of *what if* all swirled together in a cocktail I wasn't sure I was ready to drink. But for now, in this moment, with Eric's smile and Mindy's snark and Felicia's dramatics, it felt like maybe we were all going to be okay.

Or at least survive brunch.

CHAPTER

SIX

"FELICIA IS MAD AT *me*? Fuck her. She's about as relevant as a flip phone at a rave," Lexi declared, stabbing her fork into her salad. We were at our usual lunch spot—the local Olive Garden, complete with chandeliers made of wine bottles and a waiter who looked like he'd rather be anywhere else. The air smelled of truffle oil and unresolved tension.

"No, she's mad at *me*," I corrected, nudging a rogue crouton around my plate.

Lexi rolled her eyes. "Same difference. She's a human snooze button. And she dresses like a middle-school art teacher with that stupid apron. I hate her."

Claire, serene as a yoga instructor mid-savasana, leaned forward without impediment now that her bump had transformed into a full-blown baby. "Lexi, sweetie, didn't you call her a 'scheming genius' after she hacked Brody's gym schedule for you?"

I gasped, nearly inhaling a cherry tomato. "Hacked? Felicia? *Our Felicia*?"

Claire lowered her voice, as if recounting a Top Secret CIA operation. "After Brody threatened to blow up Lexi's sugar-daddy gig with Charles, Felicia went full Nancy Drew, at Lexi's behest, of course. The two had a scheme going, and a successful one, too."

"Why'd no one tell me?"

Lexi shrugged. "Forgot. Plus, you can't hide a secret like Felicia can."

Claire snickered.

"Yes, I can," I argued, but then remembered the times I'd given up Felicia's secret Tinder swipes, and shut my mouth instead.

Claire continued. "She'd text Lexi Brody's whereabouts —the full schedule, too—then Lexi'd know when to be with Charles worry-free and when Brody's schedule cleared. It was *Love Island* meets *Mission: Impossible*."

"Holy crap," I breathed. "Felicia's a double agent"

Lexi sighed, swirling her lemonade (i.e.: alcohol-free for work hours). "She volunteered. Said it 'spiced up her routine.' Pathetic, really. But useful."

"But you needed her," Claire pressed, arching a brow. "Admit it. You two were partners in crime for a little while."

"Needed is a strong word," Lexi sniffed. "More like… borrowed her proximity. Temporary. Disposable. Like those paper towels they give you at Five Guys."

The table fell silent, save for the waiter audibly sighing as he refilled our bread basket.

"Face it, Lex," I said, grinning. "You low-key love her."

"Love?" Lexi recoiled. "She's a nuisance. But fine, yes, her intel on Brody was marginally helpful."

Claire smirked. "Adorable. You're like frenemies with benefits."

"Benefits?" Lexi gagged. "The only benefit is her staying ten feet away from me. And my man."

"*Men*," Claire corrected, but Lexi just gave her a side-eye.

I couldn't blame Lexi for the venom she spat at Felicia—Felicia's habit of digging up dirt was practically in her DNA, what with her lawyer parents and a grandfather who'd been a Maryland senator. Honestly, the woman could dig dirt on the Pope with one hand tied behind her back.

"Maybe you're just angry at her for what she said about your mom," Claire observed, hitting the nail on the head.

Lexi's hands trembled slightly. "I couldn't care less what that roach thinks of me, so no, Claire. That's not it." There was an unspoken tremor in her voice—a fear of reopening old wounds, the one about her mother, the one that still haunted her. "Why is she mad at you, anyway, Eva?"

"Because I'm not buying Felicia's Tegan fan-fiction," I snapped. "She thinks I'm ignoring her, but honestly, how can she expect me to care about Tegan? That woman's been haunting my life like a bad Wi-Fi connection—always dropping in at the worst moments. And Felicia knows it! I should be charging her emotional rent for dredging this up."

Claire agreed as much, glancing up from her phone. "Ah, the Reddit drama," she said, shaking her head. "Felicia mentioned it. But between Ethan's (baby) tantrums and my Marc's (husband) newfound obsession with pickling, I've got zero bandwidth for Tegan conspiracy theories. Also, I hate her."

I threw my hands up. "Thank you! Why are we even humoring Felicia? Tegan's fine!"

"Charles would've texted me in all caps if the sky were falling. And he's got skin in the game, unlike that dope, Felicia," Lexi said. "According to him, Tegan and Scott are still posting smug couple selfies from their villa. Felicia's just bored and needs a hobby. May I suggest scrapbooking? Or therapy?"

"But the Reddit sleuths are convinced," Claire hissed. She was happy to be back into the circle of drama instead of getting it from TV soap operas. "There was a sex tape. Well —"

"—Allegedly," We all said.

"—but it vanished faster than my willpower near a cookie jar. Now they're saying Scott's crypto empire is crashing harder than a toddler on a sugar comedown. Millions in debt! Felicia says it's all linked to major fraud." She whispered the last bit like it was a government secret.

Lexi wasn't happy, however, if her twitching eye was any indication. Money talk always short-circuited her, especially when it involved her golden goose, Charles Rich. "Filthy lies!" she barked, laughing a laugh that sounded like a seagull being strangled. "The Van Hoffs could buy the moon and still have change for a private SpaceX cruise. Scott probably uses millions to wipe his—"

"I never said I believed it!" I said, tiptoeing through the conversational minefield. "But I need proof. Actual, tangible proof. Like, a spreadsheet. Or a tearful confession. Or—I dunno—Tegan herself admitting she's broke. Look, I hate her too, but I don't want her *missing*. Last week Reddit swore she'd vanished, and now she's a crypto disaster? Next they'll claim she's been kidnapped by aliens. Or worse—joined an MLM."

Lexi's glare could've melted steel beams. And suddenly, it all clicked. Why she'd been defending Tegan like a terrier guarding a hot dog.

"She won, Eva," Lexi hissed. "Tegan sauntered into the Van Hoff's vault without signing a prenup! Do you know how rare that is? She hit the jackpot without having to sell her soul to the highest bidder." She lifted a hand to stop any retort. "She's living the dream, and we're all just window-shopping, hoping it can happen to us too. So let the woman have her moment. And for Pete's sake, let her win."

"Hold on," Claire cut in, squinting like she'd just remembered her Netflix password. "Didn't we already do this 'Is Tegan missing?' chat? Or is this Mom Brain Part Two?"

I nearly snorted. Mom Brain had apparently upgraded to a subscription service.

"She's. Not. Missing." Lexi stabbed her phone screen. "Look—live from Tegan's delulu parade." She thrust the Instagram feed under our noses, her smile tighter than Spanx.

For a heartbeat, we all stared at Tegan's pixelated grin,

her caption reading "addressing the rumors." Then—*bzzzt*—the screen glitched, and Tegan's voice oozed out, syrupy and sharp as a tack.

"Don't get me started on Eva," she purred, fluffing her hair like a Bond villainess. "Total snake. Her and Lexi recently stalked me in my own home—so sick. Get a hobby, girls!"

I blinked. That's what I get for following Felicia into a snake pit.

Tegan's Instagram live rolled on, her tone now as soothing as a sandpaper massage. "Ignore the Reddit gremlins, please. Scott and I are *solid*. He's talking Paris—the drama here is nonstop—but would I let these jealous harpies chase me out? Please." She chuckled, a sound like ice cubes clinking in an empty glass. "Though if Scott buys that château… *Au revoir*, suckers!"

"That bitch," Lexi seethed, her voice dripping with enough venom to poison a village—or a *villa*. "I swear, if Tegan's 'missing,' it's only because she's hiding from her own Instagram filters. And I'm not a stalker—" She paused, jabbing a manicured finger at her phone. "Unless following this one," she pointed at me, "counts as a crime spree. Which, thanks to Felicia's Nancy Drew complex, it apparently does. Fuck me sideways."

I slumped into my chair, convinced now that Felicia had truly lost the plot. "Can we please retire 'Tegan Talk'? I'd rather discuss tax returns."

Lexi snatched up her designer tote, vintage by the looks of it. "No more Tegan. No more Felicia. I'm done. Now I've got to damage-control Charles if this news has reached him, and if he's even *slightly* frosty, I'm using Felicia's face as archery practice."

Claire and I swapped glances, watching Lexi hurry off like a bill-skipper—*which, now that I think of it—*

"Now that Lexi's stormed off," Claire announced, slapping a notebook on the table with the gravitas of a UN diplomat, "we need a plan. Eva, you're on Fix-It Duty. Get Lexi and Felicia hugging it out. Or at least sharing an Uber."

"Me?" I squawked, as if she'd asked me to wrestle a kangaroo. "Why am I the sacrificial lamb?"

"Because you're the in-between person," Claire said, tapping her pen like a judge's gavel. "Cali agrees. And Cali's never wrong—except about girl's night, obviously."

"Oh, great. Jury's in, then." Just as my existential dread peaked, my phone buzzed. Not the cheerful *ping* of a cat meme, but the ominous *thud* of Eric's text.

Eric: Café next Sat? Miss your face. And your laugh.

And… you.

Fuck me, I mean, *well…*

Normally, Eric's words would've sent me swooning like a Jane Austen heroine. But today? Today it felt like trying to parallel park a double-decker bus at peak Strip hours. I liked the slow burn, the will-they-won't-they tango… but what if I tripped over my own two feet? What if my life's chaos swallowed the romance whole?

Will I go? Obviously.

Will I like it? Absolutely.

But right now, I wanted to hurl my phone into the Bellagio Fountains and scream into a pillow until I sounded like a boiling teakettle.

CHAPTER

SEVEN

IT WAS A STUPIDLY sunny Saturday morning—the kind of day that tricks you into thinking you've got your life figured out. I'd already crushed a workout (okay, half a workout), dropped off dry cleaning I'd forgotten about since March. All that remained was a freshly squeezed OJ from the pilates studio's juice stand ($9, but worth it) and a velvety cortado at Felicia's café. Preferably with a slice of whatever tart wasn't judging my life choices. Raspberry? Lemon?

Life was so smooth, I'd almost forgotten about the Felicia-Lexi Chernobyl-level meltdown.

At Cali's.

On girls' night.

Over *mom* jokes.

The groan that escaped me could've powered a small

wind turbine. Their feud wasn't just inconvenient—it had turned our friend group into a texting war zone. And the kicker? Fixing it would've been easy if Felicia didn't ping-pong between envying Lexi's "Rich Girlfriend Energy™" and secretly admiring the author of "Gold Diggers Anonymous™."

Their drama was living rent-free—space I desperately needed for decoding Eric's latest text:"Coffee today? 11am? Miss your face."

Today. As in, *now-adjacent.*

Simple. Casual. Terrifying. Maybe it was the endorphin high from my dry cleaning victory, or maybe it was the thrill of someone actually wanting to see my un-mascara'd face. Lexi would've snorted and told me to "make him invest"—like romance was a mutual fund of emotional labor.

(Translation: "Coffee date? What is he, poor?")

And sure, part of me wanted to play it cool, to let him sweat over a *seen* receipt. But after my wobbly track record (i.e.: Fight Night Interview From Hell), I was just relieved he still wanted to see me.

Besides, we were friends.

Just friends.

Which meant Lexi's "no free emotional labor" rule didn't

apply. Right?

...Right?

Right. *Focus, Eva. Eric and his disarming smile will have to wait.*

Especially because Cali, Claire, and I had cobbled together a plan so diabolical it could've been hatched in a rom-com writer's fever dream. Not foolproof, but with a 50% chance of success (or 100% if you factored in Claire's PowerPoint slides). All we needed was for Felicia and Lexi to not rip each other's hair out.

"Oh my," Cali mumbled through a mouthful of raspberry tart, crumbs tumbling onto her blouse like confetti. "Now I see why you love it here."

"Told you," I said weakly, eyeing my own untouched slice. My nerves were doing their favorite salsa combo in my stomach, and not the fun kind. See, I was sweating it, especially because I'd fibbed to both Felicia and Lexi to lure them here—tiny lies! Harmless! Desperate times, desperate measures.

The café door chimed like the opening note of a horror movie soundtrack. *Please be Eric. Please be Eric. Please be—*

Lexi.

Of course.

She swept in like a hurricane in Louboutins, zeroing in on Felicia with a glare that could've curdled milk. "You said she wouldn't be here," she hissed, stabbing a finger in Felicia's direction.

"Lexi, please," I begged, deploying my best puppy-dog eyes. "Just be nice. For five minutes. Pretend she's... I dunno, a stranger who accidentally gifted you a stake in Meta."

Felicia, to her credit, was trying not to spontaneously combust. Sort of. She'd already death-gripped her apron like a weapon.

"Nice?" Lexi scoffed, loud enough to shake a wall. "I'm always nice. It's that *witch* who needs to be nice."

Right. Plan A: dead.

Time for Plan B.

"Ow, my tummy hurts," Cali groaned, clutching her bump with the dramatic flair of a soap opera star. I bit my lip to keep from grinning—*Oscar-worthy, babe.*

Lexi dropped her purse like it was radioactive and lunged toward her, morphing into Florence Nightingale in designer jeans. "Where? Is it sharp? Dull? Describe it!"

"Bless you, Lexi," Cali whimpered, fanning herself like a Victorian heroine. "I'm just... so sensitive to conflict. My body literally can't."

Lexi's eyes narrowed at me, sharp enough to slice ice. "Fine."

Enter Felicia, storming over like a thundercloud in an apron. "What do you want, Lexi? A gold-plated apology? A —"

"From you? I'd rather drink—"

Cali unleashed another groan, this time with a hand flourish. Lexi folded her arms, huffing. "Fine. A raspberry tart and a non-fat latte. Ice cold. And pronto."

Felicia muttered something that sounded like "Overpriced snowflake" as she flounced off.

Right. Now to keep Lexi from bolting. I pointed at Cali's stomach, channeling my inner David Attenborough. "She's tender… here."

Lexi poked Cali's belly like it was a suspicious avocado. "Is this a real medical emergency, or are you gaslighting me into bonding with Cruella de Barista?"

"It's real," Cali squeaked, doubling over like a deflating air mattress.

"Probably just trapped wind," Lexi declared, but miracle of miracles—she stayed, chatting about Cali's "stress-induced

IBS" like they were discussing the weather.

One crisis down. Now to tackle Felicia. I was mentally drafting Plan C (i.e.: Bribes? Blackmail?) when the café door chimed.

Eric.

Of course. *Now.*

I flashed him a smile that screamed "Help, I'm drowning in estrogen!" while my brain short-circuited like a toaster in a thunderstorm. How was I supposed to play peacekeeper *and* flirt with a man who looked like he'd stepped out of a *GQ* spread?

Eric, bless him, slid into a corner booth and mimed sipping a drink, his grin saying "I'll wait."

Felicia returned, slamming Lexi's latte down like a beer at Oktoberfest.

"Join us?" I chirped, patting the chair like it was a rescue puppy.

"Busy," Felicia snapped, firing a glare at Lexi that could've melted steel.

Right. Time for Plan C: prayer.

"How dare you pull that face?" Lexi hissed, jabbing a finger at Felicia like she was accusing her of stealing the last cookie. "You've been dragging me through the mud like I'm a *Survivor* villain! Do you know what it's like having my entire life—and my mom's poor choices—used as gossip fodder? I expect that from randos at the bar, but *you*?" Her voice wobbled. "You're supposed to be my friend. My human blanket on bad days—not the one chucking emotional confetti at the parade!"

Felicia's tough-girl armor clattered to the floor. She slumped into the chair like a deflated whoopee cushion. "Alright, fine!" she shouted, releasing much needed pent-up energy. "I was stressed, okay? And I know it's no excuse, but you cut deep with the mom thing."

"So do you, you know."

And just like that, the Great Feud crumbled faster than a gluten-free brownie. As they dissected the girls' night disaster, I finally exhaled. They'd survive.

Seizing my chance, I ninja-rolled over to Eric's table, dodging wayward shrapnel. Miraculously, no one noticed—too busy debating whether Lexi's mom's "stripper pole phase" counted as a workout.

Eric glanced up, his eyebrows doing that concerned-cute scrunch. "World War Three over?"

"Ceasefire achieved," I said, collapsing into the chair.

"Thanks to raspberry tarts and strategic groaning."

He grinned, that lopsided smile that always made me forget my own name. "Need to get back?"

"Soon. But I owed you a hi. Haven't seen you in ages."

"Hi," he said, softer now, and my stomach did a cartwheel. "Would like to see you more." The bruise on his brow was gone, leaving him looking annoyingly perfect— except for that yellowing bruise on his perfectly sharp jaw.

Then, casually, like he was passing the salt, he reached for my hand. His thumb brushed my knuckles, warm and steady, like a heartbeat. Not a fireworks-and-violins moment. Just… nice. The kind of nice that makes you want to write bad poetry and sing along to love songs.

And I let myself savor it. No overthinking. No panic-spiraling. Just… *Oh. This is what normal feels like.*

"I'm off to LA tomorrow," he said, "but maybe next time you can stay a little longer?"

"Maybe," I said, cheeks blazing like a sauna ad.

"I'll hold you to that," he teased, releasing my hand like he knew I'd combust if he held on longer.

I floated back to my table, where the girls were hashing out their differences.

"Okay, fine," Felicia blurted. "I'm sorry I dragged your mom's 'eccentric mating-call dance' phase into this."

"Felicia!" I blurted.

"Okay, okay. That was… uncalled for."

Lexi sighed, releasing pent up tension. "And I'm sorry I said your lack of a car makes you a 'public transport peasant.' That was… harsh."

Felicia's head snapped up. "Wait—when did you say that?"

Lexi shot me a panicked glare. "Oh. Eva didn't…? Anyway. Water under the bridge!"

"Excuse me?!" Felicia turned to me, eyes narrowing to laser precision. "You've been hoarding secrets like they're limited-edition MAC lipsticks, Eva?"

"Pot, meet kettle!" I fired back. "Remember when you 'accidentally' stalked Brody's schedule for Lexi?"

Lexi turned a shade of red usually reserved for emergency exit signs. "Shh! Eric's right there!" she hissed, gesturing to his table like he was CIA surveillance.

Cue the group snort-laughing. Felicia lunged at Lexi for a hug so aggressive it nearly toppled the syrup jar. Lexi, ever the drama queen, closed her eyes and breathed in like she was meditating at a \$200-an-hour wellness retreat.

"Claire's gonna smugly text us 'I told you so' for a week," I said, rolling my eyes.

Cali grinned. "She'll probably frame the receipt from the café as proof." Then, leaning in: "So, Felicia... any fresh Tegan gossip from your dark web forum?"

"It's a *Subreddit*," Felicia corrected, prim as a librarian. "And yes, but if I share, do not go full *Jerry Springer* on me again. My nerves can't take it."

Lexi cleared her throat, suddenly channeling Sherlock Holmes. "I did some digging too."

We all froze. Lexi + gossip = nuclear.

"Do tell," Felicia breathed, leaning in so far she nearly face-planted into a tart.

Lexi lowered her voice to a whisper usually reserved for discussing celebrity nip-slips. "Eva mentioned Scott's debt drama, so I asked Charles. He said 'Absolutely not, darling, the man's rolling in it—Google him!' So I did. And guess what? Buried under all his fluff pieces was a Reddit thread about his firm owing millions."

"*Subreddit,*" Felicia hissed, like it was any different.

"Whatever. Point is, money's missing. And you know my

motto—"

Cali blinked. "You have a motto?"

"Follow the money, honey." Lexi smirked, swirling her latte like it was a crystal ball.

Felicia slammed her palms on the table, rattling the cutlery. "See?! I *told* you Tegan's life is a house of cards! If Scott's broke, she's one bad hair day from meltdown!"

"Whoa, I'm not saying bankrupt," Lexi said, holding up a manicured hand. "But I forwarded that thread to Charles. And if there's one thing that man loves more than his vintage Rolex, it's *not* losing money."

Felicia groaned. "Please tell me he didn't invest his entire trust fund in Scott's crypto pyramid scheme."

Lexi shrugged. "If he did, we'll find him crying into his Dom Pérignon at the Wynn."

CHAPTER

EIGHT

THE RECENT TEGAN SCANDAL had us all in a tight non-asphyxiation chokehold (i.e.: Not the Tegan type.) It was like a national holiday for our group chat—brunch debates, midnight text essays, even a PowerPoint from Claire titled "Tegan's Downfall: A Retrospective." We were obsessed. Not just because her "perfect" life was actually held together by Scotch tape and wishful thinking, but because finally, the universe had yanked the mic out of her hands.

Karma, sweetie. She's a Capricorn with a vendetta.

Look, I'm not proud of the petty little thrill I got watching her spiral. Girlie was live-streaming like her life depended on it—"Eva's the villain! Lexi's a stalker! Felicia's... uh, Felicia!"—but without receipts? Honey, that's like trying to return a dress without a tag. *Good luck, babe.*

Meanwhile, anyone who'd ever side-eyed Eric Mann's viral café video (6 million views, btw) knew the truth: Tegan wasn't just a toxic friend. She was the Bowser of toxic friends. A one-woman wrecking ball in Balenciaga. And now? The internet was serving her karma on a silver platter.

About. Damned. Time.

Half her followers were shook—"Our blonde queen would Never!"—while the other half were busy screenshotting her lies like it was the *Gossip Girl* reboot. But the tide had turned. Her "trust me" schtick was crumbling faster than a gluten-free cookie. Turns out, when five ex-friends, two ex-boyfriends, and a lifeguard all confirm you're a chaos gremlin? People stop buying the angel act.

In summary? Tegan's reign of terror was over. And whose fault was that? *Hers.*

Shocker.

But here's the kicker: once we started digging into her mess, we couldn't stop. It was like online shopping at 2 a.m. *—one click, two clicks, oh god, when did I buy seven scented candles?* The worm can was open, the worms were doing TikTok dances, and we were all just... mesmerized.

Do I feel guilty enjoying her meltdown? *Pfft.* Let's just say if karma's a dish best served cold, I'm here with a spoon and a parka.

Because the truth always comes out, darling.

Especially when it's trending.

Turns out, swiping my boyfriend and getting me sacked were just *amuse-bouches* on Tegan's menu of chaos.

Case in point: A former bottle girl posted a video claiming Tegan once smashed a Champagne flute and waved it around like Excalibur. Had I seen it? No. Did I believe it? Absolutely. She once ripped a bottle girl's hair extensions because she earned more tips.

While I deep-dived into Tegan's Greatest Hits (featuring every woman she'd ever side-eyed), Lexi was playing financial detective. Not out of concern, mind—money drama is the only soap opera she binge-watches.

Instead, she unearthed Tegan's latest masterpiece: a trash-treatise about us.

"She did what?" Lexi snarled, margarita sloshing as she read Tegan's fan fiction aloud:

"According to Tegan's fan fiction, Lexi was a "low-caliber gold digger" ("I'm a high-caliber gold digger, thank you!"), I was a "jealous has-been" ("I've never *been*'!"), and Felicia was a "nosey wannabe with the vibes of a Starbucks air freshener."

Honestly? After the things *we'd* said about Tegan (erotic-asphyxiation enthusiast, bottom-tier gold digger, *sloppy thirds*), her clapbacks felt... *meh*. Like getting a passive-aggressive Christmas card from your dentist.

Lexi scrolled further, gasping. "Oh, she did not." Another gulp of margarita. "Now she's claiming she wasn't 'missing'—she was 'hiding' from me because I 'wouldn't stop begging for rich-husband tips.' *As if.*"

She flounced in the pool, sending waves splashing over Cali's floating charcuterie board. Girls' night had officially become *true crime podcast night*, and we were the tipsy narrators.

Lexi glared at her phone like it was Tegan's soul. "For the record, Charles proposed to me. With a three-carat diamond! But thanks to *her* crypto clown show, I'm rethinking it. I won't be the Duchess of Debt!" She clinked her glass against the pool edge. "TFMAM hoes stay losing!"

We cackled, knowing Tegan would've combusted on the spot.

Cali's pool was our summer HQ—part spa, part war room. The sun had finally dipped, sparing us from melting like ice pops, but instead of savoring the peace? We were three margaritas deep, Felicia's "dangerously spicy" tequila turning our brains to guacamole, still obsessing over Tegan's slow-mo car crash.

Felicia squinted at her phone. "Wait—did she just call me a… 'Reddit *Scabies*'?"

"Ooh, screenshot that," Lexi said. "Claire's PowerPoint needs a finale."

"Guys." Felicia dropped the gossip bomb like it was a grenade. "Someone found Tegan's sex tape."

The poolside chatter flatlined. Even the patio lights seemed to dim in reverence.

"Wait, that's real?" I sputtered, nearly upending my margarita into the water. "I thought that was a rumor!"

Lexi's face went full *Succession* steal-plot at a fancy dinner—tense, but trying to play it cool. "No way that's true," she muttered, snatching Felicia's phone.

Claire, ever the chaos goblin, sipped her drink. "Is this the 'Scott gets pegged' one? Lexi mentioned it ages ago. Very… Windsor-esque. William-esque?"

I choked so hard, I swear I inhaled a lime wedge.

"Claire!" Cali wheezed, clutching her stomach.

"What?" Claire blinked, innocence personified. "Lexi said it's why Scott reminds her of Prince William!"

Felicia's eyes widened like saucers. "Prince William has a

sex tape?!"

"No, but *allegedly* he's into being spanked with the Crown Jewels," Claire said, shrugging like she'd just commented on the weather.

A beat of silence. Then we howled, laughter echoing off Cali's patio furniture. *Poor Prince William.*

"Probably true," Lexi added, smirking. "Half the men in higher tax brackets pay extra for the 'royal treatment.'" She tossed Felicia's phone back. The screen was blank—another dead link. *Poof.*

"I bet they're into worse," I giggled, fully leaning into the absurdity.

"Ask Tegan!" Felicia cackled. "First choking kinks, now pegging? Next she'll say she's into tax evasion."

"There is no sex tape," Lexi cut in, her voice suddenly sharp enough to slice through the tequila fog. "Or... not one that'll ever leak."

Cali, sober as a nun at a wine tasting, zeroed in. "How do you know that?"

Lexi trailed her fingers through the water, sending ripples skittering like nervous gossip. "Because some things," she said slowly, "stay in the vault. That tape's locked up tighter than the Martha Stewart's jam recipe."

The giggles died. Even Felicia's "dangerously spicy" margarita couldn't burn through the sudden chill.

Lexi was rattled. Not "forgot her SPF" rattled. She was death rattled.

"Unless a certain cash-strapped Prince Charming decided to auction it off," Felicia said, wiggling her eyebrows like a villainess plotting over a martini—or a spicy margarita. "Desperate times, desperate *OnlyFans* measures."

Lexi's face did this twitchy thing, like a squirrel caught mid-heist with a stolen Ferrero Rocher.

"Scott's literally a human cash machine," Lexi insisted, clutching her margarita like a security blanket. "He tips waiters in Bitcoin."

"But what about that dodgy investment article *you* found?" I pressed. "Has Charles said anything?"

Lexi had forwarded the article to Charles—along with an "Explain or I'm keeping the diamond ring" ultimatum—but radio silence. (Translation: Either Charles was covering for his friend, or he'd outsourced his detective work to an intern.)

"He's ghosting me," Lexi muttered, swirling her drink so aggressively it sloshed onto her floatie. "Which means he's either clueless or lying. Either way, I'm this close to hiring a

PI named Clive with a '2-for-1' Groupon."

Cali patted her shoulder. "Truth's like a rogue Spanx wire, Lex. It always pops out."

"That's what terrifies me."

Time to lighten the mood. "Relax, the sex tape's probably lost in the cloud forever. Right next to my unsent texts to my ex."

"And if it does leak?" Lexi hissed, eyes wild. "It'll be worse than that time I accidentally 'grammed a bikini pic with visible pubes."

Claire gasped, the last of the bunch to *get it*. "Wait—do *you* have a sex tape?!"

Lexi rolled her eyes. "Obviously. Everyone in TFMAM world's got one. It's like a loyalty card scheme—swipe for free champagne! They're meant to stay locked in a vault, guarded by NDAs and shame." She lowered her voice. "But if Tegan's tape escapes… mine's just a VPN hack away."

"Fucking hell," Claire whispered, clutching her metaphorical pearls. "Is that why the links keep vanishing? Tegan's got a digital hit squad?"

Lexi nodded grimly. "Either that, or Scott is moonlighting as a cyber janitor. But until Charles texts back…" She trailed off, staring at her phone.

Felicia shot me a smug look that said "told you!." "It'll probably stay buried under a mountain of NDAs, but still—Subreddit sleuths: 1, Tegan: 0."

"They also swore she was 'missing,'" I reminded her, cringing at the memory of us raiding Tegan's villa like a drunk *Mission: Impossible* cosplay.

Felicia smirked. "True, but she *was* hiding. And let's not forget Scott's 'oopsie' with the funds, and the sex tape rumors. That's a hat trick, babe. Three. For. Three."

Before I could counter, Lexi's phone blared "Material Girl"—her ringtone for Charles. She glanced at the screen, her face tightening like a overfilled water balloon. "Gotta take this." She scrambled out of the pool, leaving a trail of drips.

"Marc and I made a sex tape once," Claire announced, casual as a weather report. "Lasted two minutes. Deleted it faster than a spam email."

We snorted, margaritas sloshing.

"Cottage cheese thighs?" Cali guessed, giggling into her glass.

"A cottage cheese *avalanche*," Claire groaned. "Places I didn't know could dimple."

The married duo cackled like witches over a cauldron of

sangria. Cali had never confessed to a tape before, but hey—after years of marriage, you either spice things up or start a pottery hobby.

The chat devolved into very detailed speculation about Lexi's hypothetical tape. "She'd look like a Bond girl!" "She'd charge for it!" All jokes, but my stomach knotted. Lexi was fraying—and not just because of the tape. Charles' radio silence was eating her alive. Tegan's dumpster-fire love life had spilled into hers, and now?

Lexi reappeared, pale as a bridesmaid dress in a mudslide.

"Holy. Shit." Her voice trembled. "Scott's emptied his accounts. He's gone. *Poof!* Vanished! And he took Tegan's dignity with him."

Silence. Then:

"No."

"Yes."

"Paris?" Felicia guessed, already Googling "private jet tracker."

"Mars?" Claire offered.

Lexi sank onto a lounger, her margarita abandoned. "Charles says Interpol's involved. And guess who's left holding the crypto bag?"

We stared.

"Us?"

"Worse. His investors. Including *Charles*."

Felicia raised her glass. "To Tegan's sex tape—may it be the *least* of her problems!"

We clinked, we laughed, we cheered.

CHAPTER

NINE

THERE HADN'T BEEN A single moment I hadn't thought about Tegan. She'd taken up permanent residence in my brain like a Netflix algorithm stuck on "Trashy Reality TV." No matter how hard I tried to evict her—blocking her Instagram, burning sage—she was inescapable. Turns out, Tegan's chaos wasn't just a personality trait. It was a lifestyle brand, and I was its unwilling VIP member.

And Scott? Oh, he wasn't just her sugar daddy husband. They were the Bonnie and Clyde of Bad Decisions—if Clyde swindled millions in crypto and Bonnie pilfered everything from VIP tables to YSL heels. The stories flooding in were wilder than a bachelorette party. A server's tip? Swiped. A rival's Audi? Keyed. A long-term friendship? Casually obliterated. The internet was having a field day, and honestly? I was too.

Las Vegas had collectively crowned Tegan its "Public Enemy *Numero Uno*," a title decided faster than you could say "all-you-can-eat buffet." The city's outrage was almost artistic—like watching Fremont Street Showgirls mob a group of tourists. Beautiful. Inspiring. A true communal masterpiece.

But just when I thought I'd hit peak obsession, Lexi dropped a bombshell over lunch.

"Charles proposed *again*," she announced, murdering her pasta with a fork. "Third time this month. Is he laundering money? Starting a cult? Or—plot twist—does he genuinely think I'd say yes?"

I choked on my strawberry lemonade. "Maybe he's sentimental?"

"Sentimental? The man uses NFTs as birthday cards." She leaned in, eyes narrowed. "This is about Scott. Charles is panicking. If Scott's empire crumbles, so does his investment portfolio. Suddenly, proposing to me is his 'safe bet.'"

"Romantic," I deadpanned.

"It's pathetic," she hissed, then paused. "...Do you think he'd spring for a no-prenup?"

"Let me guess," Claire said, stabbing her pasta. "You're wondering if Charles is another Scott-shaped grenade waiting to blow your credit score to smithereens. Obviously he is. Why else would he propose now? After months of tittering about like a man allergic to commitment? Fuck him."

She wasn't wrong. We were all furious for Lexi. Charles might not have siphoned funds into a crypto black hole, but he'd been close enough to Scott to catch the stench. And now? We were treating him like a human Glade plug-in.

"Exactly," Lexi groaned. "I've been hinting at a prenup-free wedding since Christmas—dropping clues like confetti! 'Oh, Charles, wouldn't it be romantic to marry like normal people?' 'Darling, prenups are for civilians.' But now? Now he's suddenly offering me a prenup that's basically a lottery ticket?!"

"How lottery-y are we talking?" I asked, channeling my inner LegalEagle after binge-watching three seasons of *Suits* between panic-googling "how to spot a financial sociopath."

Lexi leaned in, eyes glittering like a shark who'd smelled chum. "Ten million if he dumps me before five years. *Zilch* if I ditch him. But if we last? Half his empire. It's practically a non-prenup. A month ago, I'd have married him in a paper bag for this. Now? It's giving *desperation*."

Claire snorted. "He's panicking. Scott's gone full *Wolf of Wall Street* meets *Scooby-Doo* villain, and Charles needs a human shield. *You*."

"Exactly," Lexi hissed, shoving her pasta aside. "Tegan's out here drowning in debt, and suddenly my prenup's softer than a Cashmere cardigan? Red. Flag."

I grimaced. Tegan's "no-prenup fairytale" had curdled faster than milk in the Vegas sun, and now Lexi was side-eyeing Charles like he'd just offered her a timeshare in hell.

"Either Charles is scrambling to save his own ass," I said, swirling my straw like a daytime TV detective, "or he's romantically challenged."

"Romantically challenged?!" Claire barked. "He's a walking red flag emoji. If he proposes again, say yes—then charge him $500k just to hold your hand."

Lexi smirked, but her knuckles were white around her fork. "If I marry him, I'm hiring a forensic accountant. And a private investigator. And possibly a food taster."

"It's all about timing," Claire declared, stabbing a forkful of pasta like it was Charles's conscience. "If he'd proposed before Tegan's life imploded into a TikTok dumpster fire, maybe it'd be romantic. Now? It's like proposing during a tax audit."

Claire, queen of her "baby vomit and microwave lasagna" empire, was vibrating with rage for Lexi. It was adorable—like watching a golden retriever try to file a lawsuit.

"What if you investigate his finances?" I suggested, channeling my inner Nancy Drew (if Nancy Drew mainlined true crime podcasts and stress-ate ready-made sandwiches).

Lexi snorted. "Tegan probably tried that with Scott. These men have offshore accounts like I have lipsticks. It's a rigged game, Eva. Rigged."

"What about the sex tape?" I whispered, as if Tegan's lawyers had the restaurant bugged.

Tegan's tape was the internet's white whale—always surfacing, always vanishing. Lexi swore Tegan's team was scrubbing links like digital janitors. But why not monetize it? Lean into the "bad girl" brand? Because Tegan's ego is bigger than her Botox bill, that's why.

"Charles swears it'll never leak," Lexi said, eyes narrowing. "It's in the prenup, but I'm making him sign a separate contract. If that tape goes viral, I want a payout so big it'll make his crypto cry."

"Yes," Claire hissed, viciously twirling spaghetti. "Bleed him dry. Then buy a yacht."

I bit back a grin. Claire's life was diapers and Disney+, but here she was, ready to throw down for Lexi like a mob wife. *That's* friendship—swapping baby wipes for prenup warfare without missing a beat.

Lexi pushed her plate away, her bracelet clinking like a tiny rebellion. "If Charles thinks I'll marry him without a forensic audit, he's dumber than his NFT collection."

"Speaking of," Claire said, eyeing Lexi's untouched tiramisu, "if you dump him, can I have his wine cellar?"

My phone buzzed, and my heart did that stupid little leap it always does when Eric texts. *Chill, Eva*, I told myself, leaving it my pocket like it was a rogue *concha* I was trying to resist. But let's be real—ignoring Eric's messages was like ignoring a half-price sale at H&M. *Torture.* Still, Lexi was mid-rant about Charles' "suspiciously sudden romantic awakening," so I bit my lip and tuned back in... for approximately six seconds before caving.

Turns out, it wasn't Eric.

"Oh, crap," I hissed, slamming my hand on the table like Felicia on a gossip bender. "Felicia just sent an exposé on Scott's scam. It's live. Like, right now."

Lexi snatched my phone, her face paling to match her white scrubs. "Fuck. Me." She scrolled, her manicure tapping the screen like Morse code for "I'm doomed." "Scott's vanished, the internet's on fire, and Tegan's... what, sipping skinny margaritas in a bunker?!"

I almost pitied Tegan. *Almost.* Sure, I'd fantasized about her getting a taste of karma, but this was less "taste" and more karma force-feeding her a three-course humble pie.

"Do you think she knew?" I asked. "All that 'Blessed' Instagram drivel—was any of it real?"

Lexi snorted. "Please. Tegan could Photoshop a landfill into a Louis Vuitton pop-up. But this?" She waved my phone like a prosecutor with a smoking gun. "Scott's been playing chess while she was playing Snapchat."

Claire leaned in, eyes wide. "How did Charles not sniff this out? He's meant to be Sherlock with a Amex Black Card!"

"No. Idea." Lexi stood abruptly, slinging her purse over her shoulder. "But I'm about to audit his soul. Claire, cancel my patients. This is an emergency."

As she stormed out, Claire muttered, "At least it's Tegan's life imploding, not ours."

"Yet," I added, watching Lexi bail the restaurant like it was on fire.

My phone buzzed again.

Eric: "Miss you. Coffee soon?"

I sighed. Right now, Tegan's meltdown was the main act, and we were all just popcorn-munching spectators.

But hey—at least the view was entertaining.

CHAPTER

TEN

THERE WAS LIFE BEFORE the scandal, a blissful blur of lattes and low-stakes drama. And then there was life after. It was like being trapped in a group chat with a thousand hyper-caffeinated tabloid editors—constantly buzzing.

The news didn't just break; it oozed, dripped, then exploded like a rogue champagne bottle at a garden party.

Tegan, our resident human tornado, was back in the spotlight—but this time, it was less "red carpet" and more "dumpster fire." The internet, ever fickle, had swapped their #BossBabe emojis for pitchforks. Sure, a few die-hards still defended her ("She's misunderstood!" "Scott's the real villain!"), but let's be real: schadenfreude tastes better with popcorn.

Felicia and I were knee-deep in the mess, but I told

myself it was research. Noble, selfless research—to protect Lexi from becoming "Tegan 2.0: Debt Barbie." If a few scandalous morsels fell my way, well, *bon appétit*.

"A hundred million dollars, Eva!" Felicia gasped, clutching her laptop like it held the nuclear codes. We'd been holed up in our shared apartment for hours, surrounded by empty chip bags and the glow of our screens. "Scott didn't misuse it—he yeeted it into a crypto black hole! This isn't embezzlement; it's performance art!"

I nodded, half-listening, as I cross-referenced a Subreddit thread titled "Tegan's Tax Evasion Wardrobe—A Thread." The Subreddit had become our holy grail—a chaotic mix of armchair detectives and unhinged conspiracy theories. Think murder podcast meets Insta baddies.

Felicia, meanwhile, had rebranded herself as "The Nancy Drew of Nouveau Riche," complete with a faux detective hat she'd swiped from a Halloween display two years ago. "I'm essential," she declared, zooming in on a pixelated screenshot of Scott's offshore accounts. "Lexi needs a prenup and a background check. I'll charge Charles hourly—in champagne."

"Or exposure," I quipped, dodging a thrown Hot Cheetos.

"Exposure pays in followers, babe. I accept Visa."

The Subreddit sleuths were thriving, of course. They'd gone from speculating about Tegan's "mysterious disappearance" to dissecting Scott's LinkedIn endorsements. ("He's 'Skilled in Strategic Investments'? More like 'Skilled in Strategic Exit Strategies!'")

But Felicia's crowning achievement had been unearthing a photo of Tegan's "borrowed" YSL heels—mid-theft—blurred but damning. "Exhibit A," she crowed.

"You're wasted at the café," I said, scrolling through a thread titled "Is Tegan's Dog a Crypto Wallet?"

"Tell me something I don't know," she sighed, then paused. "Though, to be fair, I did accidentally serve a cappuccino with a side of stalking. Customer loyalty cards are just begging to be mined for data."

We both knew the Subreddit wasn't infallible—their "Tegan's Sex Tape" hype had fizzled faster than a Diet Coke left open—but Felicia's confidence in the basement dwellers was unshakable. She'd gone full *CSI: Las Vegas*, and I was just here for the snacks.

As the clock ticked past midnight, I wondered if we'd crossed the line from "concerned friends" to "obsessed weirdos."

But let's be real: mainstream media's "investigative journalism" was about as deep as a puddle in July. They'd recycle the same three "exclusive" facts—Scott's rich! Tegan's not! Drama!—while the Subreddit? *Baby.* The Subreddit was out here playing chess while the tabloids played *Snakes and Ladders.*

These amateur sleuths had cracked Scott's financial empire wide open—unearthing shell companies, dissecting trust funds, and piecing together his courtship with Tegan like it was a *Where's Waldo?* of red flags. They'd even dug up their wedding certificate, which, frankly, I didn't know you could do. But Felicia said what's public information is easily attainable. It was like the FBI outsourced their work to a book club hyped on espresso martinis.

(Note: Uber Eats espresso martinis next cyber recon?)

And the wildest part? The Subreddit loved Tegan. Like, *loved* her. They'd turned into her unpaid legal team, scouring that prenup for loopholes like it was a *Sunday Times* crossword. "Look! Clause 4.2! If Scott invests in crypto post-wedding, Tegan gets a yacht *and* a formal apology!" Bless their spreadsheet-loving hearts.

Meanwhile, the haters slithering into the threads? "Gold-digger!" "Go back to serving cocktails!" But Tegan's fans swatted them away like gnats at a garden party. "She's a victim, you monsters!" they'd cry, flooding the feed with hashtags and eventually block the haters. Girl had a fan army bigger than the BeyHive, and they were committed.

Was it creepy how easily strangers mapped her life? Absolutely. These people knew Tegan's Starbucks order (venti oat latte, extra foam, side of regret) better than their own moms. But hey, if a Subreddit thread titled "Scott's Offshore Accounts: A PowerPoint" could save her from bankruptcy, who was I to judge?

"Oh, great—this one says it's half a billion," I said, squinting at my phone like it had just confessed to murder. We'd read so many articles about Tegan and Scott's dumpster fire, I could've written a dissertation titled How to Ruin Your Life in 10 Easy Steps (feat. Crypto). The media had rebranded Tegan from "Cinderella in Louboutins" to "Wicked Stepsister of Wall Street," and honestly? The plot twists were wilder than the Lost finale.

The narrative was clear: Scott was basically a posh pirate, hunting for a bride dumb enough to marry him, inherit his debt, and let him vanish into the sunset with a solid gold parachute. Sure, his family's fortune was still intact (ugh, nepotism), but his personal trust fund? Frozen faster than a Ben & Jerry's pint.

But let's be real—nobody knew what was true and what was inflated click bait. One article screamed "Millions gone!" The next wailed "Billions—yes, with a B!" The Subreddit tried to decode it all, but honestly, it was like watching toddlers explain quantum physics. "NFTs!" "Blockchain!" "Tax evasion in space?!"

All we knew? Scott was a con artist with a Rolex, and Tegan was his accidental accomplice—less Bonnie and Clyde, more Botox and Bankruptcy.

Felicia nudged me, her brow furrowed. "How's Lexi coping? She's gotta be eyeing Charles like he's a ticking time bomb, yeah?"

"Pfft. She's furious. But get this—Charles just drafted a new prenup. Basically hands her his empire if he so much as sneezes wrong."

"Silver linings!" Felicia chirped, though her smile faded. "Shame Tegan's life is now a *Daily Mail* comments section."

She wasn't wrong. Tegan's "happily ever after" had curdled into a "holy *shit* ever after," and Lexi's "I told you so" echoed louder than a YouTube announcement. "Slow down!" she'd warned. "Don't do erotic asphyxiation on the first date!" she'd begged. But Tegan? Too busy Instagramming caviar towers to notice the cliff edge.

Lexi played the game like a queen of the *slow burn*. While Tegan dove into Scott's arms like she was cannonballing into a gold-plated pool, Lexi made Charles sweat. She'd drape herself over chaise lounges, sip martinis with glacial poise, and drop hints like, "Darling, Van Cleef is so… commitment-y, isn't it?" until Charles folded faster than a house of credit cards. Both women craved the glitz, but Lexi made him earn it—one vintage jewel at a time.

"Tegan's cooked," I said, scrolling through another headline screaming "From VIP To RIP." "But Lexi's flirting with Brody harder than a $2 vodka shot? Is she hustling Charles or eyeing the exit?"

Felicia snorted. "Lexi? Settle for middle class? Please. The woman treats her Porsche like a firstborn child. Brody's a fling—a distraction to make Charles grovel harder."

"Can't grovel lower than a no-prenup-prenup. But Brody hasn't even had a fight since Eric's knockout," I said, though secretly I wondered if Lexi kept him on speed dial just for the thrill of making Charles' eye twitch or for a raunchy bedroom thrill.

Felicia leaned in, her grin morphing into something downright *schemey*. "Speaking of Eric… When are you climbing that man like a jungle gym?"

I choked on my iced tea. "Felicia!"

"What? You've been eyeing his biceps since the café incident. Don't think I didn't see you drooling when he came last time."

My cheeks flamed. "Okay, fine—I admit it! I've mentally drafted a very detailed itinerary for our first romp in the sheets, but don't tell anyone!"

"Eva!" she singsonged, clinking her glass to mine. "But I support this delusion. Text me immediately post-coitus. I need scandalous specifics."

We cackled, Tegan's drama momentarily forgotten—though I knew it was only a matter of time before her name trended again in our apartment. Lexi's prenup victory lap, Eric's biceps, Felicia's Subreddit sleuthing... Our lives were as messy as our friendships.

But for now? Let Tegan's mess simmer. We had priorities.

CHAPTER

ELEVEN

SATURDAY MORNINGS WERE MY sacred ritual—a sweaty, endorphin-pumping pilgrimage to the altar of Pilates, followed by an iced cortado at Desert Bloom that tasted like liquid air conditioning. Sure, Las Vegas in July felt like standing in a hairdryer's blast zone, but today? Today, I was *glowing*. Not just from the workout, but from the miraculous alignment of the universe: my crop top hadn't ridden up, my hair had defied sweat to form a casually chic low bun, and my gold hoop earrings stayed put thanks to Lexi's genius Band-Aid hack. I looked like a TikTok thirst trap, if the trap was set by someone who considered "hydration" a personality trait.

The café hummed with its usual chaos, but today the air smelled spicy. And not just because Felicia had accidentally doubled the chili in the breakfast omelet. No, this was the scent of *drama*. The Tegan scandal had fizzled out like a damp firework, replaced by a fresh, steaming cup of gossip: Misty Mindy's very complicated love life.

"Mindy's gone full *Love Island*," Felicia hissed, sliding my cortado across the counter. "Princess Mimi found out she's been texting some MMA girl from Pahrump, and now it's war. Yesterday, Mimi threw a protein shake at her head."

I nearly spat out my coffee. "Princess Mimi?"

"Yeah, Mindy's girlfriend. Mindy's trying to turn their relationship into a polyamorous situation, but Mimi's not sharing the spotlight. Or the Wi-Fi password."

It was gloriously messy. Mindy, who once convinced me she and Eric were a sure thing, was now at the center of a love triangle so tangled, it needed a flowchart. And if Princess Mimi was anything like Mindy, she fought like she was starring in a telenovela directed by Guy Ritchie.

"Remember when we thought Mindy was Eric's mystery girlfriend?"

I groaned, cringing at the memory. "Turns out she's just everyone's mystery girlfriend."

Felicia grinned. "Speaking of Eric—when's he back? You've been eyeing his Instagram like it's a cookie jar."

"Next week," I said, refusing to blush. "And I'm not 'eyeing' it. I'm researching. For science."

"Science?" Felicia arched a brow. "Babe, the only 'research' you're doing is figuring out if his 'gym selfies' are shot in natural lighting or a Calvin Klein dressing room."

I opened my mouth to protest, but—well. She wasn't wrong.

As I sipped my cortado, I marveled at the café's magic. However wild life got—Tegan's crypto meltdown, Mindy's MMA melodrama—it all circled back here. Like *Cheers*, but with more almond milk and passive-aggressive smoothie names.

Felicia leaned in, eyes sparkling. "Want to hear the real tea?"

"Always."

"Princess Mimi's moving in with the Pahrump girl. They're pulling a *Game of Thrones* and pushing Mindy out of the 'thruple' that never was."

I gasped. "No."

"Yes." She nodded to the counter, where Mindy was giggling over a matcha latte with Shane, the always-late barista. "Place your bets now: How long till Mimi storms in with a nunchuck?"

We snorted, and I retreated to my usual table—the one with the wobbly leg and a view of the outside trees. But alas, my book was MIA. I'd forgotten it, once again. Sad! Tragic! Sighing, I jammed in my AirPods and queued up Eric's latest podcast: "Grappling With Success: A Fighter's Guide to Vulnerability." His voice oozed through the headphones, warm and gravelly, like a cashmere blanket dipped in whiskey.

Felicia appeared with my cortado and tart, arching a brow at my dreamy expression. "You're listening to him, aren't you?"

"Research," I lied, sipping primly. "He's discussing… um… the emotional complexity of arm bars."

"Sure, hon. And I'm the Queen of Pahrump—*fucking hell*," Felicia gasped, nearly launching my tart into orbit. I yanked out my AirPods, whirling around just as Tegan stumbled into Desert Bloom like a disgraced Bond villain who'd missed her cue.

"Tegan?" I echoed, my sunny mood evaporating faster than a puddle in the Vegas heat. There she stood—normally polished to a high-gloss finish, now resembling a shampoo commercial before the "after" shot. Her hair? A tumbleweed dipped in platinum-blonde dye. Her eyes? Swollen into puffy slits, like she'd ugly-cried through a *13 Reasons Why* marathon. Even her mascara had given up, trailing down her cheeks in defeat.

It was jarring, seeing her so *un*-Tegan. She was never anything less than camera-ready—even her gym selfies had better lighting than my wedding photos (if I ever had any). But here she was, a human Pinterest board gone rogue.

"Eva," she croaked, her voice trembling like a Jell-O mid-mouth-flight. "Can we talk?"

My heart did a guilty little somersault. *Why now?* I'd just perfected my "casually aloof" vibe for Eric's imminent arrival. But saying no to Tegan in this state felt like kicking a kitten. In Louboutins.

"Of course," I said, gesturing to the chair Felicia had already sanitized twice.

Felicia, bless her, vanished faster than a Diet Coke at a Weight Watchers meeting, muttering, "I'll bring... things. Cake. Sprite. A vat of concealer."

Tegan slumped into the seat, shrinking like a deflated party balloon. I opened my mouth to say something— anything—but before I could muster a "So... crypto, huh?" the café door swung open.

In sauntered Eric Mann, looking like he'd just stepped off a Men's Health cover shoot. *Of course.* His biceps glistened under the café lights, and his smile hit me like a rogue serotonin blast. We'd planned to "casually bump into each other" next week, but fate—or Felicia's meddling—had other ideas.

Then he spotted Tegan.

To his credit, Eric didn't gawk. Instead, he pivoted to the counter with the grace of a man who'd dodged literal punches, pretending to study the menu like it held the meaning of life. ("Today's Special: Existential Crisis Panini.")

Tegan buried her face in her hands, muttering, "I look like a ghost from hell, don't I."

"You look… fine," I offered, cringing internally.

She snorted—a wet, unglamorous sound. "Fine's overrated."

Felicia reappeared, slamming down a cortado, a lemon tart, and a croissant the size of a toddler's leg. "Eat," she ordered Tegan. "Carbs are cheaper than therapy."

As Tegan picked at the pastry, Eric shot me a discreet eyebrow raise from across the room. "You okay?" it said. I nodded, mouthing "Later," and he grinned—a tiny, private promise that made my stomach flip.

Tegan glanced between us, her puffy eyes narrowing. "So that's happening, huh?"

"Shut up," I said, but I was smiling.

"And god, look at me," Tegan sniffled.

It wasn't lost on me that she'd once swiped my boyfriend faster than a contactless payment, but seeing her now—mascara smudged, extensions sticking out like a deranged halo—was like watching a designer handbag get run over by a bus. Tragic. Fascinating. But mostly tragic.

"Let's bail," I said, tugging her arm gently. The café was buzzing louder than a group chat after a scandal, and the last thing Tegan needed was to trend as "Crying Crypto Bride (Gone Wrong)."

"Where… where are we going?" she whispered, sounding about as confident as I do trying to parallel park.

"My place," I said, shooting Eric a "Not now, hot stuff" glance over my shoulder. He gave me a subtle nod—part knight-in-shining-armor, part "I'll spot the cortado later."

If you'd told me months ago that Tegan "Blessed" Van Hoff would be slumped at smy IKEA kitchen table, guzzling Felicia's mom's "Divorcee's Tears" iced tea (recipe: 50% lemon, 50% spite), I'd have laughed until my Spanx snapped. Yet here we were.

The AC hummed like a zen monk, and Tegan clutched her mug like it held the secrets of the universe. She'd swapped her designer disaster for Felicia's unicorn pajamas ("They're ironic!" Felicia insists, lying), and honestly? She looked better. Less "reality TV meltdown," more "toddler after a tantrum nap."

Her face was still puffy—think overripe peach—but makeup-free Tegan had a raw, human vibe. Nothing like I'd ever seen from her before.

"I'm sorry," she blurted, staring into her tea like it was a crystal ball. "For… you know. The… stuff."

The stuff. Ah, yes. The "stuff" where she'd swiped my boyfriend and got me fired, the "stuff" where she pretended to be Eric's boo thing and made me spin my wheel the opposite direction. The "stuff" was practically endless when it came to her.

But watching her nibble a full Oreo sleeve with smeared mascara down her face, I couldn't muster a single zinger. Not even a "Karma's a latte, huh?"

Instead, I passed her the whole packet. "Eat. Felicia's mom says sugar cures 80% of life's problems. The other 20% require wine."

She snorted—a wet, unglamorous sound—and for the first time in years, I saw the girl who'd once drunk-dialed me at 2 a.m. to PhD-level discuss *My Big Fat Gypsy Wedding*. Not the Tegan who'd hijacked my life, but the one who'd hijacked my lip liner in junior year.

"Are you okay?" I asked, not knowing what else to say. Tegan responded with a sob so loud, it could've drowned out a jet engine. Felicia shot me a look that screamed, "This is your mess to deal with. I'm just here for the Oreos."

We didn't need words. The unspoken truth hung in the air. Tegan—*the* Tegan—was now a sniffling puddle on my sofa, clutching my years-old "Team Edward" chipped mug like it was a lifeline.

I'd be lying if I said part of me wasn't smug. *Karma's got a PhD in petty,* I thought, recalling the Subreddit threads dissecting her downfall. But seeing her mascara migrate south to her chin? Less schadenfreude, more "Oh, honey, did your eyelashes file for divorce too?"

Felicia broke the silence with the grace of a bulldozer. "Right. Iced tea's not working. Should I open the vodka? Or a beta blocker infused cupcake?"

Tegan peered up, her face a Picasso painting of despair. "C-can I stay here?" she whispered, like a deflated balloon.

Sorry? My brain short-circuited.

But then... *ugh*. Her trembling lip. The way her chipped

manicure tapped the mug. She looked about as threatening as a soggy croissant.

"Why me?" I blurted, channeling my inner rom-com heroine. "You've got, like, 1.2 million 'besties' online. Can't one of them lend you a yacht?"

"They blocked me," she hiccuped. "Even my dog's Instagram went private, the threats were terrible."

Felicia snorted. "Dramatic. But relatable."

Tegan's shoulders hunched further. "Eva, I've got no one. My DMs are just *crickets*. And my lawyer's invoice has more hits than my wedding album."

Felicia mouthed "yikes" over her tea.

I sighed.

Tegan's eyes pooled with fresh tears, and she let out a noise halfway between a hiccup and a deflating balloon. "I'm so sorry, Eva. You're the only one who hasn't blocked me. And I don't blame them, honestly—I'd block me too."

"*You* blocked me!"

"I mean in *real* life!"

I sighed, my inner Girl Scout battling my inner Vindictive Ex-Friend. *Be the bigger person*, I told myself, while mentally billing her for emotional labor. "What do you need? A hug?

A lawyer? A really strong shot?"

Felicia, perched on the arm of the sofa like a judgmental flamingo, chimed in. "Or we could call Lexi. She's basically the human equivalent of Google for rich-people disasters."

"Genius," I said, whipping out my phone. "Lexi'll have this sorted by nightfall."

"No!" Tegan lunged for my phone. "Lexi's one of *them*. She'll feed me to the tabloids!"

I blinked. "Tegan, darling, Lexi's the only one who can help you."

Tegan flopped back onto the sofa, muttering about "trust" and "gold diggers" while I dialed Lexi.

Three hours, two pots of tea, and one cryptic text later ("On my way. I'll bring wine."), Lexi swept in like a hurricane in an Hermès scarf.

"Darling," she said, eyeing Tegan's mascara streaks with the disdain of a art critic at a preschool finger-painting exhibit, "we've got work to do."

Felicia grinned. "Told you she'd help."

And just like that, the Tegan Rehabilitation Project™ began—with Oreos, scheming, and a very expensive bottle of something French.

CHAPTER

TWELVE

MY APARTMENT WAS WHAT real estate agents generously call "compact" and I call "perfectly sized for avoiding step counters." Cozy? Absolutely. If by "cozy" you meant that Felicia and I could high-five each other from opposite sides of the room without spilling our rosé. But Tegan? Tegan surveyed the space like it was a prison cell designed by IKEA.

"Eva's apartment is adorable," she said to Lexi, her tone dripping with the same enthusiasm one might reserve for a moldy salad. "But how long can a person live here before developing a vitamin D deficiency? I'm used to natural light, darling. And walk-in closets. Multiple walk-in closets."

Felicia nearly choked on her shortbread cookie. "Oh, pardon us, Princess Tegan. Should we sprinkle gold leaf on your Trader Joe's hummus? Fluff your pillow with endangered bird feathers?"

Lexi, ever the diplomat, tossed her Chanel clutch onto the sofa like a grenade. "Babe, if you'd prefer a park bench, I'm sure Eva won't mind."

I bit back a laugh. Watching Lexi and Felicia team up to eviscerate Tegan was like witnessing two rival drag queens spontaneously harmonize. Magical. Terrifying.

Truthfully, I hadn't seen Felicia and Lexi agree on anything since that time they both swore off men (for 45 minutes). But here they were—united in their disdain for Tegan's diva antics. Baby steps? More like baby *stomps*.

Still, the air buzzed with unresolved tension. Felicia side-eyed Lexi's new "I'm rich but relatable" outfit, while Lexi pretended not to notice Felicia's "accidental" spillage of herbal tea on her designer jeans. I hovered between them like a UN peacekeeper armed only with shortbread.

"Lexi, *please*," Tegan whined, flopping onto the sofa. "Your penthouse has a hot tub. And Charles' credit card. He owes me after Scott's little vanishing act."

Ah, yes. Scott's "vanishing act"—a phrase that undersold the drama like calling the Titanic a "pool mishap." He'd left Tegan with debt taller than her hair extensions and fled to a tropical island, presumably to start a crypto-themed juice cleanse.

Lexi arched a brow. "My penthouse isn't a charity for ex-wives of financial Houdinis. But if you'd like, I'll ask him to comp you a night at the Four Seasons. *One* night. And only if you promise not to steal the towels."

Felicia snorted. "Or the mini-bar."

"Or the doorman," I added.

Tegan pouted, but even her pout had lost its shine, like a pig left out in the rain. For a split second, I almost felt sorry for her. "I don't like it here."

Lexi's head snapped around like she'd just spotted a spider in her Birkin. "Excuse you?" she hissed, her voice sharp. "One more word, and I'll personally book you a one-way ticket to Delulu Land. Try me."

Tegan, ever the uninvited houseguest, groaned, picking a rolled pill on the couch. "It's just so small, Lexi. Eva's shower could double as a phone booth. And don't get me started on the lack of ambient lighting."

Felicia choked on her tea. "Ambient lighting? *You're* ambient lighting? Eva's letting you crash here rent-free, and you're critiquing our dimmable bulbs? No wonder karma's your roommate."

Lexi barked a laugh that could've shattered champagne

flutes. "If you want a penthouse, hop on Tinder and find a new crypto bro. Or better yet—Dubai's lovely this time of year. I hear yacht girls get free Botox."

Tegan gasped, clutching a throw pillow like it was a life raft. "Yacht girls? Lexi, that's vile. I'd rather sell my soul to a Timeshare demon!"

"Then quit whining," Lexi said, tossing her hair. "My place is off-limits, and if you diss Eva's 'cozy chic' one more time, I'll donate your designer luggage to a woman's shelter. With tracking."

I'd finally hit my limit. "Tegan, my place is small, but my patience is smaller. You've got till sunrise. Then you're Airbnb-ing a park bench."

Her face crumpled. "But the Wynn blacklisted me! My Gucci slides can't handle pavement!"

"All I hear is *wah-wah-wah*," I said, mimicking a tiny violin.

Felicia fist-bumped me. "Savage."

Tegan gaped, her lip quivering. "You're kicking me out? Into the desert heat? I'll *melt*."

"Pack sunscreen," Lexi said, snapping a selfie like Tegan was tourist attraction.

"Greedy anaconda," I muttered under my breath,

watching Tegan slither across the sofa like a disgraced reality star having a toddler-level fit.

"You *have* to let me stay with you, Lexi," Tegan wailed. "My credit cards are frozen! I can't even order a smoothie without triggering a fraud alert!"

Lexi snorted, sipping her tea with the calm of a woman who'd just been asked to donate a kidney to a stranger. "Darling, if I let you within ten feet of my penthouse, you'd swipe the silverware and flirt with my doorman. Hard pass."

I stifled a laugh. Lexi's condo was Fort Knox with a side of marble countertops. I'd seen her old one once, briefly, while picking up an outfit—a "strictly five-minute visit" that involved signing a waiver and leaving my shoes at the door. Tegan had better odds of hacking the White House.

"Prioritize, Tegan," Lexi added, scrolling through her phone. "We're hunting Scott's trust fund, not booking you a spa day. Though God knows you need one."

Lexi's motivation was clear: money was her love language, and unraveling Scott's financial maze was her idea of foreplay. If she ever faced a Tegan-level disaster? She'd have six exit strategies, a burner phone, and a Swiss bank account before the first tear dried.

Felicia, meanwhile, had morphed into a Subreddit ninja, curled on the sofa with her laptop glowing like the

Washington Monument. "These Reddit sleuths are legends," she murmured, eyes darting. "One guy traced Scott's crypto to a meme account called DogeDad69. Another found Tegan's wedding playlist—'Single Ladies' was track three."

In the kitchen, chaos reigned. Tegan was stress-eating hummus straight from the tub, Lexi was barking at a lawyer named Jones ("Find the loophole, or I'll find a new lawyer!"), and I was Googling "how to evict a human hurricane."

"This is hopeless," Tegan moaned, flopping onto the counter. "I'll be living in Eva's shower until Christmas!"

"My shower," I said, "is the size of a toaster oven. You'll have to Airbnb a kid's closet."

Lexi snapped her fingers. "Focus. We need a loophole. A… financial Hail Mary."

Felicia suddenly gasped. "Guys. The Subreddit found a shell company called 'Van Hoff's Happy Fun Time LLC.' Registered to a PO box… in Pahrump."

We stared.

"Pahrump?" I whispered. "That's where Princess Mimi lives." It didn't matter, but it was an observation.

"You need a lawyer," Lexi declared, slamming her palm on the table like a judge sentencing a ham sandwich to life without parole. "This isn't a game, Tegan. We can't hashtag our way out of financial fraud."

Tegan sniffled into a napkin that had "Girls' Night 2022: Wine Not?" printed on it. "I don't want a lawyer. I want my marble bathtub back! And my husband! Well, maybe not the husband. But definitely the bathtub."

Lexi snapped her fingers so sharply, I half-expected a flock of doves to scatter. "Focus. Scott didn't marry you without prenup because you're *soulmates*. He did it because you're a human shield for his crypto circus. Now, we're finding receipts, or you'll be couch-surfing till Christmas."

Tegan wilted like a supermarket orchid. "But he said pegging was romantic—"

"Second date, Tegan!" Lexi groaned, massaging her temples like they owed her money. "Even my stripper mom knew to wait till dessert before breaking out the handcuffs!"

Felicia, meanwhile, sat statue-still on the sofa, her laptop glowing into the growing night. Normally, she'd be cackling at Lexi's "I told you so" symphony, but today? Crickets.

"Felicia?" I nudged, eyeing her suspiciously. "Did you unearth Scott's secret Bitcoin account?"

"That dumb Subreddit again?" Tegan sneered. "It's just basement-dwelling keyboard warriors cosplaying as FBI agents. They know nothing about me."

Felicia didn't flinch, but her fingers froze mid-click. Her face paled to match the café's oat milk latte aesthetic. I plopped onto the sofa beside her, eyeing her screen like it held nuclear codes. "What's wrong?"

Felicia's voice dropped to a horror-movie whisper. "Eva. It's… the worst thing that can pop up right now."

My heart sprinted like it was training for a marathon it hadn't signed up for. "What thing?"

Lexi peered over her blue-light glasses, smelling drama like a truffle pig. Tegan stomped over, her slides clacking like a metronome set to panic. "Whatever it is, I've already lived it. Spill."

"Don't," Felicia hissed, clutching her laptop to her chest like it was a newborn. "Eva, grab it! She'll literally combust!"

But Tegan lunged, her manicure flashing like a wrestler's championship belt. "Give. It. Here!"

A brief tug-of-war ensued—Felicia's "Live Laugh Love" laptop case vs. Tegan's "I've Never Apologized in My Life" energy—until *click*.

Silence.

Tegan's face drained faster than a bathtub with no

stopper. Lexi leaned in, squinting. "Oh, fuck. Is that…?"

Felicia buried her face in a cushion. "The sex tape."

There it was. Glowing on the screen: Tegan and Scott, mid-romp, in what appeared to be a gold-plated room.

"Why is there a giant painting of a peacock?!" Lexi barked, fixating on all the wrong things.

Tegan made a noise like a deflating balloon animal. "That was our honeymoon suite! Scott said it was artistic!"

Felicia peeked one eye out. "It's gone viral. The Subreddit's calling it 'Birds of a Feather Get Naked Together.'"

"Delete it!" Tegan wailed, flinging the phone like it was cursed.

"Too late," Felicia mumbled. "It's already a TikTok sound."

Lexi sighed, pouring herself a very large drink. "Well, look on the bright side. At least he's wearing socks."

CHAPTER

THIRTEEN

CALI'S POOL WAS ABOUT as refreshing as a lukewarm bath, but I dunked myself anyway, clinging to the illusion of "self-care" like a koala to a eucalyptus leaf. The sunset painted the sky in Hot Mess Pink™, and the margaritas flowed like liquid optimism—though mine tasted suspiciously like Felicia's "experimental" mix of tequila and lime electrolyte powder. ("Hydration is key, Eva!")

Girls' night trudged on, blissfully Tegan-free. Of course, Tegan had popped into my life, but not girls' night (Translation: Too paranoid to face Cali's wrath), yet desperate enough to haunt my apartment.

Cali, usually a one-woman tribunal when it came to Tegan's crimes (stolen boyfriends! sabotaged jobs! casually shitty person!), was now sidelined by the sheer logistics of being 30 weeks pregnant. "I'd hex her," she muttered, waddling past with a plate of nachos, "but I can't bend over to light the candles."

Tegan's downfall had become a global spectator sport. Her face was everywhere—tabloids, TikTok thirst traps, even a very questionable cameo on a true-crime podcast titled "Gold Diggers & Crypto Vigilantes." Her "fans" (a mix of bored keyboard warriors and aspiring BossBabes) had turned her into a martyr with merch lines and hashtags. JusticeForTegan trended twice before breakfast.

And Scott Van Hoff? The man was a ghost. A rich, tanned ghost sipping mojitos on a yacht named "Asset Protection." The internet dubbed him "Scamthony Hopkins" after someone unearthed his cringeworthy poem about "disrupting the blockchain."

The whole saga was a fairy tale gone Fyre Festival—equal parts mesmerizing and tragic. Everyone wanted a front-row seat to the meltdown, preferably with a side of guac.

"Pass the dip," Lexi said, scrolling through Tegan's latest Instagram post—a cryptic selfie captioned "Trust the Journey." "She's literally using a filter called 'Glamorous Grief.' I can't."

"At least she's consistent," Felicia replied, knee-deep in the Subreddit's latest theory: "Scott's Secret Twin: A PowerPoint." "Remember when she called Eva's car a 'tragedy'? Now she's hiding in it."

I sipped my margarita, savoring the chaos.

Scott's financial dumpster fire had officially gone viral. The Van Hoff dynasty—once the poster family for "old money chic"—was now trending for all the wrong reasons. If Scott "Crypto Casanova" Van Hoff could embezzle millions while maintaining his combover, what other sins lurked in the family vault? Cali, ever the conspiracy theorist, was convinced they'd been hexed by a "generational wealth curse." "Money's like a chocolate fountain," she said, "too much and you'll drown in the brown."

"I can't believe she's moaning about your apartment again," Claire spat. "The gall of that woman! You've given her a roof, Wi-Fi, and three types of hummus. She's living rent-free in your life *and* your couch!"

I shrugged, half-smiling. Claire's outrage was oddly comforting—like a human chihuahua barking at my bad decisions. Yes, Tegan generally sucked, but kicking her out now felt like abandoning a feral cat in a thunderstorm. A very high-maintenance cat, with a highlights reel of betrayal.

"Today she said the sofa gave her 'texture trauma,'" Felicia announced, air-quoting. "Texture trauma! Babe, this isn't the Four Seasons—it's IKEA's 'Sandpaper Chic' collection. And remind me, who's the one eating chips in *my* pajamas?"

Cali snorted, rubbing her bump like a crystal ball. "Guests are like sushi, Eva. Fresh for 48 hours, questionable by day three, and utterly toxic by day six." She paused. "Also, I'm 90% sure she's using your toothbrush."

"What'd I miss?" Lexi breezed back in, heels clicking like she was the belle of the ball, though we all knew her fourth "bathroom break" was really a covert Facetime with Brody. (Honestly, the woman had the subtlety of a glitter cannon.) I'd bet my last gum they were plotting a tropical escape— white sand, sunset romps, and zero mention of prenups or pilfered trust funds. Lexi would spin it as "karmic revenge" on Charles for... existing, probably. Never mind that Charles had dodged her ring-shaped ultimatums like a man allergic to platinum.

"Just agreeing that Tegan's gone full *Eau de Trash Panda*," Claire said, swirling her marg with a smirk. "Six days on Eva's sofa, and she's marinating in her own regret."

Lexi flopped into a chair, eager to gossip. "Rude. But true. Though Trent's taking her case, so brace yourselves— she'll be back in Balenciaga by Christmas."

Trent, Lexi's legal attack dog (and occasional whiskey connoisseur), was the human equivalent of a wrecking ball in a Savile Row suit. If he'd agreed to sue the Van Hoffs for "emotional distress," Tegan might actually win enough to buy a small island—or at least a very forgiving PR team.

"Good," Claire declared. "She put up with Scott's TFMAM (Trust Fund Middle-Aged Man) act, only to learn he was just… MAM (Middle-Aged Manboobs)!"

Felicia nearly spat out her electrolyte margarita. "From trust fund dreamboat to discount kayak. Worst glow-down since Fyre Festival."

"Let's not downplay her role, either," Claire added, wiggling her eyebrows. "The pegging? The asphyxiation? The sex tape with literal mood lighting? Girl earned that settlement like an Olympic sport."

"It's not like the sex tape is any good," Felicia said.

A chorus of "Nooo" erupted. Felicia turned the color of a sunburnt tomato.

Lexi slammed her glass down, scandalized. "None of you better be watching that tape! It's a violation! And also—why is there a peacock painting?"

The room fell silent, the gravity of Tegan's global humiliation hitting us like a rogue piñata. For a heartbeat, I almost felt… sorry for her. Then I didn't.

Sympathy: 1%.

Desire to never share a bathroom again: 99.9%.

"I'm sorry!" Felicia gasped, clutching her glass like a life raft. "I thought it was one of those strategic leaks! You know, like when Kim K 'accidentally' drops a hairbrush and breaks the internet? I just assumed Tegan was pivoting to spicy influencer!"

Lexi's eyes narrowed to laser precision. "Strategic? Babe, this isn't a brand deal—it's a *crime*. That tape's about as consensual as a tax audit. If we so much as breathe about it online, we're basically funding digital pickpockets. And I will personally haunt you." She shuddered, her Chanel earrings quivering with moral outrage. "Sends shivers up my spine."

I nodded solemnly, though privately I wondered if Lexi's fury was partly fueled by the fact her own "tasteful footage" with Charles was stored in the Cloud. ("It's for posture reference!")

Claire, ever the chaos gremlin, grinned. "Lucky Tegan. My sex tape would be rated 'Napping Mom: The Snorequel.'" She gestured to her postpartum leggings, stained with pureed carrot and defiance. "Though maybe if I get that mommy makeover, I'll start an OnlyFans. 'MILF & Cookies.' Patreon tiers include nap tutorials."

"Claire," I laughed, nearly spilling my drink. "You'd break the internet."

Felicia, eyes sparkling with mischief, pivoted to me. "But Eva—imagine you and Eric! UFC fighter meets girl-next-door? You'd be the Beyoncé of OnlyFans. 'Eva & Eric: Submission Only.'"

"Felicia!" I screeched, hurling a cushion at her. She dodged, cackling like a witch who'd just hexed a parking meter.

My cheeks burned hotter than a jalapeño. Eric and I had been toeing the line between "will-they-won't-they" and "why-haven't-they-yet" for weeks. Every text he sent—"Miss your laugh"… "This podcast guest reminds me of you"—was basically emotional kerosene. If Felicia kept fanning the flames, I'd spontaneously combust before our first date.

Lexi smirked, swirling her drink. "Relax, Eva. If you two ever do make a tape, just ensure the lighting's flattering. And maybe avoid peacock-themed décor. Aesthetic matters."

The group erupted, and I buried my face in my hands. Tegan's scandal? Global humiliation. My love life? A very chatty group text.

"I saw them at Desert Bloom last Saturday," Felicia announced, wiggling her eyebrows like a mischievous parakeet. "Eva and Eric were practically undressing each other with their eyes. If the café had a broom closet, they'd have christened it. Twice."

"Would not!" I spluttered, my face flaming hotter than an oven. "We literally bumped into each other! And then Tegan arrived, wailing about her life like a canceled Karen asking for forgiveness. There was no time for eye contact, let alone —"

"Sure," Felicia drawled, miming a tiny violin. "Just like Lexi and Brody 'accidentally' bumped into each other at the Palms rooftop bar. What's next? A coincidental weekend in Malibu?"

The room erupted in gasps. Lexi's electrolyte marg sloshed perilously close to the edge of her glass.

"Felicia!" she hissed. "I told you that in confidence! You're about as discreet as a dumb parrot!"

Cali, perched on the sofa like a pregnant Buddha, finally interjected. "Hold on—Eva's dating Eric, Lexi's banging Brody, and *no one* thought to loop me in? I'm gestating a human here! Do you know what sleep deprivation does to my FOMO? I'll cry into my decaf latte!"

"She's not wrong," Claire sighed, nibbling a guac chip with the gravity of a philosopher. "Pregnancy turned me into a human sprinkler. I cried because Trader Joe's was out of hummus that last week. Hummus."

I seized the chaos to pivot. "Lexi. Are you actually dating

Brody? Why am I the last to know?"

Lexi rolled her eyes. "Oh, please. You've been too busy *not dating Eric* to notice."

"Says the woman who's ghosted Charles for a man who thinks 'asset portfolio' means Instagram gym selfies!" Felicia retorted, toeing the line between cheeky and Chernobyl.

Lexi's gaze turned arctic. "Felicia, babe, tread carefully. Or I'll revoke your access to my nice girl mood."

Desperate to defuse the tension, I threw a distraction. "What's the latest with Charles, then?"

Lexi sighed, twirling a strand of hair. "Since the Tegan fiasco, he's been obsessed with locking me down. Prenup's gone softer than a supermarket avocado. But honestly? I'd rather date a Roomba."

"You deserve better than Charles," Cali said, rubbing her bump sagely. "Maybe Brody's... different?"

"Brody?" Lexi snorted. "Babe, Brody's fun, but he's about as financially stable as a baby in a onesie. And his UFC career? Let's just say his greatest strength is his hair gel."

The room dissolved into laughter—the kind that bubbles up like champagne and leaves your cheeks aching.

Felicia raised her glass. "To accidental eye-sex and

terrible life choices!"

"Felicia!" we chorused, clinking anyway.

Because really, what's a girls' night without a little chaos?

CHAPTER

FOURTEEN

THE SUN BURNED ON, doing its best impression of a vengeful hairdryer, and I could practically feel my four-month-old Botox waving a white flag. *Sun wrinkles incoming!* I thought, squinting into the glare. But between Tegan's diva demands and the Everest-sized luggage pile in my hallway, my collagen levels were the least of my worries.

After weeks of Tegan treating my apartment like a pop-up purgatory—complete with daily critiques of my "peasant cutlery" and "barbaric" sofa—Felicia and I had finally cracked. We'd staged an intervention over two-day guac and very strong vodka, informing Tegan it was time to "embrace her inner phoenix" (i.e.: *skedaddle*). Miraculously, her frozen funds had thawed just enough to book her a one-way ticket to Anywhere But Here.

"I can't believe you've survived this long without a proper

silverware," Tegan sniffed, tossing another sequined jumpsuit into a suitcase large enough to house a small family. "And these walls—are they deliberately the color of despair?"

Felicia, hauling Tegan's third Louis Vuitton trunk down the stairs, muttered, "Next time she complains, I'm 'accidentally' donating her to Goodwill."

Tegan had arrived with seven suitcases and a PhD in passive aggression. She'd insulted my dying fern ("Is it supposed to look suicidal?"), my eccentric mug collection ("Charming. If you're into tacky art"), and even the air ("Does your AC filter hate you?"). Now, as she packed, she'd unearthed more designer gear than a Kardashian garage sale.

"Need help with the other 12 suitcases?" I asked sweetly, holding up a shoebox labeled "Shoes (VIP Bottle Girl Edition)."

"Don't be dramatic, Eva," Tegan sighed, as if I were the one traveling with a portable walk-in closet. "This is just the essentials."

Felicia caught my eye, mouthing "essentials?!" while miming a noose.

"Jesus H. Christ, what's in here? Bricks? *Gold* bricks?" I grunted, heaving Tegan's suitcase down the stairs like Sisyphus with a gym membership. The July heat was doing its best to melt my willpower—and my four-month-old Botox.

"She's lucky we're not charging her a 'diva tax.'"

Felicia wiped sweat from her brow, scowling at the suitcase now teetering on my car's bumper. "I could've been serving lattes to normal people today. Instead, I'm playing pack mule for Princess Prada."

My seven-year-old wheezed as I crammed the luggage inside, its suspension sighing like a boomer at a Zumba class. The irony wasn't lost on me—Tegan had once called this car "a tin can with commitment issues," yet here it was, ferrying her Gucci-laden life to greener pastures.

"Do you think Lexi'll lend us her Porsche?" Felicia whispered, eyeing the five remaining suitcases with dread. "These look like they're smuggling bodybuilders."

"Not a chance," I said, just as Lexi materialized behind us, sunglasses perched like a Bond villainess.

"Scratch my car, and I'll scratch you," she said, tossing Tegan's monogrammed tote into the trunk.

Tegan pouted, deploying her signature "wounded kitten" face. "Lexi, *please*—just one teensy favor? Your Porsche has so much more space—"

"Oh, honey," Lexi cut in, voice sharper than a stiletto. "That pout works on men who think 'NFT' stands for 'Nice Fun Time.' Not on me. Call an Uber."

Tegan stomped her foot, her Valentino slides smacking the pavement. "You're all so mean. I'll just do it myself!"

"Tegan, babe, the world's exhausted by your Oscar-worthy dramatics," I said, fanning myself with a crumpled In-N-Out receipt. The sun was baking us like two slightly stale croissants, and my patience was melting faster than Tegan's waterproof mascara. "Keep this up, and you'll be solo again —just like in high school after you stuck gum in Jaime Luna's hair. Or that time you 'accidentally' stole the tennis bracelet and blamed me for it. Or—"

"Alright, Eva!" she snapped, swatting the air like my words were wasps. "Must you dig up ancient history? It's been years. Let it go, or you'll need a brow lift instead of Botox for your frown lines."

The sunlight caught her face, forcing her to squint like a disgruntled meerkat. *Brow lift, who?*

"Then explain this," I said, getting the courage to ask some burning questions. "Why'd you lie about Eric that snowy night? The snow, the Tesla snub, the 'Oh, Eva, we're soulmates' bullshit?"

Her gaze dropped to her manicure—chipped, I noted with petty satisfaction. "I didn't think it'd blow up the way it did. I just… wanted him."

"Oh, brilliant! So you thought, 'I'll torpedo Eva's love life and blame the snow'?"

"*No.* You always make it about *you*," she groaned, flipping her hair. "I liked him, okay? I wanted him. Then I saw him looking at you like you'd invented air, and I—I snapped. You've always had this… thing. Like the universe hands you a golden ticket while I'm stuck with scratch-offs."

I barked a laugh. "A golden ticket? Tegan, I drive a gaudy green car that smells of sour milk stains. My life's a Groupon for chaos."

She dabbed her neck with a tissue, sighing like a melting whoopee cushion. "For the record, nothing happened with Eric. I just wanted you to think it did. Ruin him for you. Petty? Sure. Effective? Obviously."

"You *are* a fucking liar," I hissed, going in for a slap.

Tegan caught my wrist, her toned arms flexing with infuriating ease. "Stop it, Eva."

Fucking Pilates.

"You're just smoke and mirrors in Valentino slides."

"Guilty," she shrugged. "The truth is Eric never wanted me. Not even when I 'accidentally' texted him that photo of me wearing nothing but a smile. Turns out, he's gay." She paused, grinning bitterly. "Tragic, really."

I ignored her comments. "Why confess now?" I snapped.

"Sudden attack of conscience? Or did your karma app finally ping?"

"Please. I heard you and Felicia giggling about his biceps in the bathroom. Figured I'd rip off the Band-Aid before you two start doodling 'Mrs. Eva Mann' in glitter pens."

"Tegan!" Lexi bellowed from the stairs, sounding like a disgruntled drill sergeant. "Get your annoying ass up here before I auction your luggage on Poshmark! And Eva—" She added, as an afterthought, "—stop being so… *Eva*. It's not a crime, but it *is* annoying."

I huffed. Tegan puffed.

"Tegan! Now!" Lexi roared, punctuating her demand by "accidentally" nudging a suitcase down two steps.

Felicia wedged another trunk into my car and whispered, "Jealousy's a disease. Eric chose *you*. That's her villain origin story."

"This started *way* before Eric," I said, watching Tegan wrestle a suitcase shaped like a small continent.

Tegan chimed in. "Eva, you're just so easy to hate. If you weren't you, you'd hate yourself."

"So you hate me now?"

"No! It's just a saying."

"Oh, spare us the martyr act, Tegan," Lexi drawled, inspecting her nails after dragging another luggage. "Let's dissect your iconic villain arc, shall we? One: You swiped Eva's boyfriend not because you liked him, but because you could. Classic narcissist. Two: You got her fired from the lifeguard gig because her tan was better. Tragic, *womp womp*. Three: Flashing your Amex like it's a personality trait? Babe, even my grandma's Spanx have more subtlety."

She paused, flicking an imaginary speck off her. "And let's not forget your *pièce de résistance*: Scott. You married a human trust fund just to flex, didn't you? But then—" Lexi's grin turned razor-sharp, "—along comes Eric, who'd rather watch Eva reheat leftovers than take you to Nobu. *Devastating*. You're the blonde bombshell, and she's the little Mexican girl who outshone you without even trying. You expected him to overlook her just like you overlooked her, but he didn't. He fell right into her honey trap. Bet that stung like Sprite up the nose."

Tegan gaped, her face paler than a January detox smoothie. "You have no idea what you're talking about," she spluttered, clutching a suitcase like a life raft.

Lexi snorted. "Please. You're as transparent as Shein leggings. Now hop in your Uber before I charge you for the emotional labor."

I stared at Tegan, the puzzle pieces clattering into place. "All this time you hated me because you thought you were better than me? Over my skin color?"

"It's not about your skin color," she snapped, rolling her eyes so hard I heard her eyelashes creak. "It's about… I don't know what it is. You've got this… thing. Things are just easy for you. I have to scheme for mine!"

"Ah yes, your 'scheming.' AKA grand larceny and felony tax evasion," Felicia chimed in, throwing a tube of lip balm into Tegan's trunk. "Here—for when you inevitably charm another billionaire. Minty fresh lies, babe."

Lexi yawned, texting with one hand. "Wrap it up, T. Your suitcases are giving main-character energy, and we're all just extras in this telenovela."

Tegan huffed, wrestling a trunk into the Uber like Cinderella post-curfew. For once, she was speechless—a miracle rivaled only by my car surviving another summer.

As the Uber vanished, Lexi turned to me. "Feel avenged?"

"Dunno," I said, eyeing the leftover luggage. "But I *do* know her Birkin's fake."

Felicia grinned. "Next time she visits, let's change the Wi-Fi password."

CHAPTER

FIFTEEN

WEEKS HAD PASSED SINCE Tegan flounced out of my shoebox-sized apartment and into her own place—a "temporary solution" she'd said, though we all knew it was a studio the size of a Target cart with a bathroom that smelled vaguely of despair. But hey, it was funded by Scott's rapidly dwindling accounts, so in her books, that counted as a win. Never mind that Scott's idea of "funding her lifestyle" had once included ski trips to Aspen and a Birkin bag she'd accidentally left at the café. Now it meant microwave meals and a mattress she'd haggled from Facebook Marketplace. Progress, right?

(Translation: Less gold digger, more *penny pinching*.)

Not that Scott was winning any awards either. The man had more legal drama than a *Suits* marathon—fraud charges, shell companies, the works. But Tegan? She'd outsmarted him with the one thing he'd never seen coming: a sugar baby contract.

Yep, you read that right.

Back when they'd first met—him in his Saville Row suit, her in a "VIP bottle girl" sequin dress she'd nabbed from a flash FashionNova sale—she'd had the foresight to sign a lucrative sugar baby contract. Salon budget included. Whether it was a luck of the draw (greedy Tegan) or consciously money savvy (Tegan, CPA), it saved her ass when the lawyers came sniffing.

Turns out, she'd been smart enough to quietly funnel his cash into her personal accounts during their 2007-Era-Britney-Marriage (Translation: Lasted less than a year). Embezzling from your own husband? Bold. But her legal team—slicker than a greased penguin—argued it was just "contractual obligations" and she'd done her part of the deal. "Services rendered," they called it, straight-faced. The judge, bless him, actually bought it. Or maybe he just pitied her for having to live with Scott's habit of leaving wet towels on the bathroom floor—or the pegging thing. Either way, the courts let her keep the cash.

Meanwhile, Scott's gone full *Where's Waldo*—last spotted, "meditating" in St. Barts while his empire crumbled. *Allegedly*. Tegan's lawyers are spinning her as the clueless

Vegas girl who married a conman, while the prosecution reckons she's his Bonnie without the Clyde. No prenup, though, so technically, his mess is her mess. Unless, of course, she can prove he once used her favorite mascara on his Star Spangled Starfish. Then it's war.

Lexi says a win's a win, even if it's dodgy-er than a 3 a.m. taco. Me? I'm just here with popcorn, waiting to see if Tegan's next move involves a tell-all memoir or a *Love Island* cameo. Cheers, Scott—you fucking bastard.

Tegan hadn't just landed on her feet—she'd stuck the dismount like an Olympic gymnast, complete with a gold medal in How To Glow Up After Your Husband's Empire Implodes. Not only had she thawed her frozen bank accounts, but she'd also transformed her new apartment into a showroom for "Budget Versailles." How? No idea. Witchcraft? A *Queer Eye* meets *The Craft* crossover episode? All I knew was, when Lexi dragged me over for a visit, I half-expected a butler named Carson to offer me a monogrammed towel.

Last time we'd tracked (fine, *stalked*) Tegan down, she'd been living at the very fancy—if a tad geriatric—Wynn Villas. Now? She greeted us from her Target-cart-sized apartment with a charcuterie board arranged à la Martha Stewart and rosé so chilled it could've frostbitten my fingers. *Slow progress?* I thought, more like *speedy recovery.*

(Translation: It's all a mindset, babe.)

The apartment was *stunning.* Like, *Home & Design* "Before and After" stunning. I mentally screenshot every detail—the gilded mirrors, the rug, the velvet chairs that whispered, "Sit on us and instantly become interesting." I was ready to stage a PowerPoint intervention for Felicia on "Why Our Place Shouldn't Look Like a Laundromat's Sad Cousin."

But Felicia, ever the rebel, just shrugged. "Marble countertops are cold," she said, loyal to our saggy sofa and the coffee table I'd DIY'ed from a door, splinters and all. And honestly? She was right. Our place smelled like cookies and bad decisions. Tegan's smelled like regret and credit card debt.

The real shocker, though? Tegan and Lexi were now *besties.* Yes, those two—formerly locked in a silent war over who'd snatch the most return out of their TFMAM. Turns out nothing bonds people like mutual disdain for the same bankrupt conman. Lexi swore Tegan was "inspirational," if you ignored the minor details (embezzlement, a fugitive husband, boyfriend swiper—the works).

"She's proof you don't need a man to ruin your life!" Lexi chirped, sipping Tegan's bargain bin rosé. "You can do it yourself with poor decisions and sheer audacity!"

Meanwhile, Charles—Lexi's is-he-or-isn't-he-fiancé-turned-doormat—was still paying for her luxury condo, her Porsche payments, and what I suspect was a clandestine Raya account. He'd finally caved on the prenup (too late, buddy), but Lexi had already gone off him.

Lexi had gone full Top Secret about her TFMAM lately —tight-lipped, cryptic, and probably communicating in Morse code. Charles, her once steady flame (wallet), now smoldered like a forgotten candlewick beside Brody, her shiny new man with washboard abs. She'd been soft launching him on socials, a blurry beer-in-hand here, a partial floating fork there. Meanwhile, Charles was rolling into an early grave trying to get Lexi back.

But Lexi had already swerved into her next plot twist. And for once, it wasn't a man, a prenup, or a suspiciously sudden inheritance from a "long-lost uncle." Nope—this time, it was *Tegan*.

Claire nearly choked on her endless salad. "So… you're quitting the clinic?"

"Not yet!" Lexi said, though her tone screamed "See you later, losers!" "But imagine—Tegan's got the followers, I've got the hustle, and Brody's got the cheekbones for the ad campaign."

"But I'm going to miss you!" I whined.

"*Pfft*, I'll make it work!" Lexi declared, waving her lemonade like a magic wand. "Between my grueling medical career, my flourishing social life, and my newfound passion for serums that smell like post-existential crisis, what's one more thing? Time management is my love language, babe."

Their newfound Sisterhood Of The Gold Digging Pants had spawned a business idea—a skincare line called Dewy & Damaged™. "It's authentic," Lexi explained, twirling her cajun pasta like she was conducting an orchestra. "Part skincare, part therapy, all tax-deductible. And you—" She pointed her fork at me. "—are our first influencer. Congrats! Start posting thirst traps ASAP."

Claire's smile was tighter than a Spanx waistband, her "calm" as stable as her mom brain.

"A skincare line," I repeated slowly, as if Lexi had just announced she'd taken up lion taming. "With Tegan."

"Obviously," Lexi said, leaning in like she was sharing state secrets. "Her scandal's hotter than a jalapeño right now. People live for a redemption arc! Claire—" She swiveled to face her, "—you're our 'Hot Mom' ambassador. Stretch marks? Perfect. We'll call them 'life stripes.'"

Claire blanched. "Marc will think I've joined a cult."

"Good! Controversy boosts engagement. Speaking of—" Lexi's eyes glittered, "—Tegan's sex tape? We're leaning in. Our first product's 'Afterglow Balm'—for when life gets sticky."

I nearly spat out my lemonade. "Lexi!"

"What? The video's got 2 million views! That's free market research."

Claire buried her face in her hands. "I'm going to have to explain this to my baby when he's old enough, aren't I?"

"And your mother-in-law!" Lexi chirped. "Viral marketing, Claire! Think of the possibilities!"

Claire groaned, covering her face with a breadstick.

"It's not like we're inventing the wheel. The Kardashians did it with Kim—now they're basically the royal family of Instagram," Lexi said, gesturing with her fork like she was conducting a TED Talk on scandal monetization. "And Paris Hilton *invented* the whole 'leak-and-profit' strategy. Tegan's just following in their exhibitionist-for-pay footsteps."

"Oh my god, Claire," I said, my brain still buffering. "Are we really comparing Tegan to Kim Kardashian? Kim's got a billion-dollar empire. Tegan's got a sex tape and a dodgy ex-husband."

"She's right, though," Claire cut in, nodding sagely.

"Controversy is currency, babe. And Tegan's sex tape is trending harder than a cat video. We'd be mad not to cash in —even if I have some explanations to give."

"Really Claire? They got you so easily?"

Claire, ever the voice of cautious optimism, added, "I mean, if you think about it, the exposure could actually help sell skincare. People love a comeback story. Especially if it comes with a free sample of 'Afterglow Balm.'"

"I mean, she does look amazing," Lexi admitted, swirling her straw like she was pondering the mysteries of the universe.

"Wait, you *watched* the sex tape?" I gasped, horrified. "I thought we were actively avoiding it!"

"I caught, like, five seconds," Lexi said, shrugging. "But then Scott came into frame, and I noped out faster than you can say 'eye bleach.'"

"Same," Claire chimed in, shuddering. "I lasted until the awkward heavy breathing started. Then I closed the tab and ate an entire tub of ice cream to recover."

"Unbelievable," I muttered. "Here I was, thinking we had standards—collectively. And you got so mad at Felicia, too."

Lexi shook her head, swallowing a bite of salad. "It's not

the same. I watched it because Tegan's talking about licensing it. Felicia, on the other hand, saw it the moment it dropped. Like, before Tegan even knew it existed."

"Exactly," Claire said, nodding like this was a perfectly normal conversation to have over lunch.

"Felicia's over that little hiccup," Lexi said, waving a hand dismissively. "Just tell her she's on the PR list, and she'll be too busy posting selfies to care."

But Claire, ever the buzzkill, wasn't letting it go. "Not to be that person, but… how can you trust Tegan after what she did to Eva? The very many things, in fact."

Lexi didn't miss a beat. "She's not going to screw this up. She's got nothing left—no friends, no money, no dignity. This is her last Hail Mary. She's not risking it."

"So you trust her because she's desperate?" I asked, raising an eyebrow. "Or are you just giving up on Charles and a prenup-free wedding fantasy?"

"A bit of both, no?" Claire said thoughtfully, tapping her chin. "If you wanted to be controlled by Charles and his trust fund, you'd have married him by now. But you didn't. Which means one thing—you've finally realized your own power, haven't you?"

Lexi grinned, clearly delighted. "Exactly," she said,

leaning back like she'd just solved world peace. "It's empowering. I've never felt this good about a decision before. And honestly? It's addictive."

"So," I said slowly, "what's next? A reality show? A memoir? Tegan & Lexi: The Musical?"

Lexi's eyes lit up. "Don't tempt me."

CHAPTER

SIXTEEN

"ONE ICED CORTADO AND a lemon tart," I announced, excitement bubbling.

It was Saturday, and my insides had morphed into a full-blown Cirque du Soleil—complete with trapeze-artist butterflies, a clown car of nerves, and a popcorn stand labeled What If He's Forgotten My Face? Honestly, the emotional overhead was exhausting.

"Isn't Eric back today?" Felicia purred.

I batted my lashes. "No idea what you're talking about."

"Oh my god," she hissed. "You little minx."

Eric and I had been texting for weeks while he hopped around the Sates, doing podcasts and photo ops after his UFC win transformed him from "that hot guy who gyms two doors down" to "hot guy with a Wikipedia page." Proud?

Sure. But mostly, I was just counting the minutes until he'd stop being a concept and start being a person I could share an awkward moment with.

I collapsed into my usual window seat, eyeing Desert Bloom's "botanical oasis"—a trio of succulents that looked less *desert paradise* and more *desert apocalypse*. Normally, I'd dive into a book, but today? My focus was shorter than the lifespan of a TikTok trend.

"Someone's got a case of Eric-*itus*," Felicia trilled, materializing beside me like a milk-stained fairy godmother.

"Do not," I muttered, as my stomach did a backflip that would've scored a 10 at the Olympics. Any moment, Eric would stride in, sweep me into a rom-com kiss, and—

"Hey, bitch," Lexi bellowed, torpedoing into the chair next to me. "Why do you look like you just won the lottery and snorted coke?"

"I do not," I said, my cheeks now matching the emergency exit sign.

"Whatever. Brody's making me meet him here. Again. At 10 a.m., like I'm not a human being with a skincare routine. Charles would've booked a spa."

"Relax! At least the coffee's good."

"It's quaint," Lexi sneered, as if "quaint" meant "haunted

by the ghost of a disgruntled barista." "If Brody thinks I'm hopping across town for non-fat lattes without a *hefty* brunch bribe, he's thicker than his protein shakes. And let's be real— he's no Eric. That man's wallet's probably got its own zip code. Too bad the dick is good. I'd be more apt to say no, yet here I am."

"Lexi!"

"What? If the dick's good, the commute's worth it. That's my motto."

"I thought you said a hefty bribe?"

"Well, no bribe yet I'm here, aren't I?"

"Please don't embroider that on a tea towel."

"Tegan's already mocked up merch. We're calling it the 'D Train Collection.'"

I was a human espresso shot, my nerves tap-dancing in my stomach, while Lexi scrolled through her phone like she was single-handedly propping up Instagram's stock price. I, meanwhile, was melting into the chair like a popsicle in a sauna, trying not to hyperventilate.

"Your cortado and lemon tart," Felicia announced, plonking the plate down. I stared. This wasn't a tart—it was a Michelin-starred daydream. Strawberries glistened like they'd been polished by tiny fruit butlers, and the edible flowers were arranged with the drama of a *Bridgerton* ballroom. It belonged in a museum. Or at least on *Bake Off*.

"Jesus H. Christ," Lexi muttered, eyeing it like a seagull eyeing a fry. "That's not dessert, it's a flex."

Before I could even whisper "mine," she'd flagged Felicia and barked, "Same for me—and make it snappy. I've burned more calories today side-eyeing Brody's texts than I did in spin class."

Felicia grinned, while Lexi speared a forkful of *my* tart. "Just a bite," she lied, swiping a bite the size of Texas.

I opened my mouth to screech "That's practically assault!"—when the café door banged open. And there they were: Eric and Brody, sauntering in like they'd just walked off a *Men's Health* cover shoot, all smirks and biceps and *oh god why is Brody wearing a tank top*?

My stomach executed a full backflip. There he was—Eric, in actual human form, looking less like a mortal and more like he'd escaped a Tom Ford ad. His eyes locked onto mine, and suddenly, the entire universe shrunk to the size of a 2 a.m. DM. That gaze, hot as the Vegas sun. That smile that could melt a tub of Ben & Jerry's in seconds.

"Finally," Lexi barked, shattering the moment with the subtlety of a kazoo solo at a funeral. "Ten. Minutes. Late. Brody. Do you know what I could've accomplished in ten minutes? I could've deep-conditioned my hair, drafted a passive-aggressive email, and stalked my ex's new girlfriend. But no. Here I am, hangry and tart-less, because *someone*"—she jabbed a finger at Brody—"thinks 'flexible scheduling' means 'whatever Brody wants.'"

Brody shrugged, muscles rippling like a Marvel sidekick. "Babe, you want me to be the next Conor McGregor? Sacrifices must be made."

"Yeah, *your* sacrifices, not *mine*. Now, pay up." She thrust her hand out and Brody pulled his wallet out like a regular Joe and gave her crumpled up bills that likely accumulated to $7.

I shot Eric a look that screamed, "Really?" and he sent one right back, so I kept my mouth shut.

So much for my fantasy of a slow-motion rom-com reunion—complete with a spinning camera angle and a Mariah Carey impersonator.

As Lexi and Brody devolved into their usual squabble—"No, Brody, $7 isn't enough!"—Eric slid into the seat beside me. His presence was like slipping into a bubble bath after a day of troubles: warm, calming, and mildly suspicious.

"Hi," he said.

"Hi."

Before I could say "I thought I'd imagined you," Felicia swooped in like a popup. "Replacement tart for the victim," she announced, plonking a new plate in front of me. "And for the tart bandit," she added, sliding Lexi a slice with a glare.

I thrust the fork at Eric, offering him a bite. Shockingly, he leaned in and took it, his lips grazing the fork in a move that should've come with a parental advisory warning. The smirk that followed wasn't just a smirk—it was a whole situation. My hand trembled like a chihuahua in a snowstorm, but then Eric's hand landed on my knee under the table, warm and steady. Just like that, I melted. Being near him was like swapping Spanx for pajamas at midnight—blissful, uncomplicated, and borderline indecent.

"Holy hell, that's lethal," he said, licking his lips.

"Told you."

I briefly fantasized about Lexi and Brody being teleported to a silent retreat in Siberia. Instead, they were locked in their usual routine: 30% arguing, 70% foreplay, 100% mortifying.

Eric and I weren't talking, but the eye contact? It was speaking *War and Peace*—director's cut. Naturally, Lexi pounced.

"Shut up, Brody," she snapped, stopping his rant about "spinning back kicks" or whatever nonsense his gym-bro brain had latched onto. She pointed between Eric and me like she'd just caught us rocking a confession booth. "What's happening here?"

Cue the silence.

Brody squinted between us, forehead creasing like a confused bulldog. "Wait—*this* is your big homecoming surprise?" he barked at Eric. "I thought you swore her off for jumping to conclusions! And that bad interview!"

My brain short-circuited. *The bad interview?* Since when did Eric have opinions about my *bad interview*?

Before I could implode, Lexi cackled like she'd mainlined laughing gas. "Eva's the queen of jumping to conclusions," she crowed. "And secrets, too, since she's been hiding whatever's happening here?" She flapped her hands at us like we'd spontaneously combusted.

Eric's ears turned pinker than a strawberry Frappuccino, and good Lord, it was so unfairly endearing.

"I do *not* jump to conclusions," I protested, even though, deep down, I knew Lexi had a point. (Okay, fine, *several* points. But I wasn't about to admit that.)

Lexi smirked. "Should we leave, or do you two need a room? Because that look is smoldering." She burst into laughter, and I seriously considered throwing my tart at her.

"We're just friends," I said quickly, but the heat creeping up my face was basically screaming, Liar! I just knew I was blushing through my sun-kissed tan.

"Really?" Eric said, his voice warm and steady, like he'd been waiting for this moment. "Because I was hoping we could be more than friends."

My heart did a somersault (10! 10! 10!). Across the table, Lexi and Brody gasped in unison, then immediately dissolved into laughter, clearly enjoying my utter meltdown.

"The timing hasn't exactly been in our favor," Eric continued, his tone softening. "With the fight and, well, the other stuff." He glanced at me, acknowledging the messy circumstances that had kept us apart. "But I'm back now, and I'm here to stay. So, please, say yes. Go out with me—if you'd like, that is."

I couldn't speak. Couldn't breathe. I was melting faster than an ice cream cone in July.

"Holy shit," Felicia said, appearing at the table like she'd been summoned. "Did I literally just walk in at *peak* drama? Because Shane took forever with the cappuccinos—we had to remake them, like, three times—but wow. Eva, say *yes*."

She dropped off everyone's drinks, but I barely noticed.

Eric was watching me, his expression equal parts hopeful

and nervous. Around the table, my friends were practically vibrating with excitement, like they'd all just won the lottery (and snorted coke).

"I would love to," I finally said, my voice barely above a whisper.

Lexi let out a victorious cheer, and Felicia clapped her hands together like she was at a Broadway show. "Little Eva is no longer single! Finally!"

I was still blushing—there was no hiding it—but when Eric reached for my hand, that familiar rush of nervous excitement settled into something steadier. My heart was still racing, but the fear that had been lurking beneath it all started to fade.

"So, does this mean we can talk shit about Tegan in front of you now, or no?" Lexi asked, barely giving me a second to process what had just happened. "Because I have some news, and I'd rather not wait until you leave."

"Say it now," Felicia urged, glancing at her watch. "I have to get back to work soon."

Brody snorted. "Better get used to this," he said, nudging Eric. "They can go on and on about nothing."

Eric just smiled, completely unfazed. Like he didn't care what we talked about—he was just happy to be here.

"Tegan's sex tape is officially out," Lexi announced, her voice dripping with the kind of glee usually reserved for Black Friday sales. "She gave in and got it licensed—apparently fighting it in court would've cost more than her Louboutin collection. Plus, she told me *millions* of people have already watched it. At least now she's getting paid."

"Tegan has a sex tape?" Brody's eyebrows shot up so high they practically disappeared into his hairline.

Lexi smacked his arm. "You're not allowed to watch it."

"Wouldn't want to anyway," he said, rubbing his arm where Lexi smacked it.

Eric just shrugged. "Not my thing."

Felicia wrinkled her nose like she'd just smelled something foul. "Scott's in it, so I doubt anyone's lining up for a front-row seat. And it's mostly Tegan pegging him, so… yeah, hard pass. Scarred me quite a bit, actually."

I stifled a laugh, but now I couldn't unsee that mental image. *Thanks, Felicia.*

"So, how rich is she exactly?" Felicia asked, leaning forward like she was about to hear the juiciest gossip of the century.

Lexi leaned back, smirking. "She got a lump sum upfront, but she's also getting royalties on every sale. She's set for a while."

"Good. That means she won't be coming back looking for handouts," Felicia said, looking visibly relieved.

"Even better," Lexi added, her grin widening. "Because she's funding our skincare line. She's basically our sugar mama now."

Felicia snorted. "So, she's your new trust fund baby?"

Lexi narrowed her eyes. "I am my own trust fund baby, thank you very much." With Brody's crumpled $7, I believed her.

I jumped in before they could start bickering. "It's for their skincare line, Fel. I told you—we're on the PR list."

Eric raised an eyebrow. "A PR list? Doesn't that mean going public? Because I remember how long it took just to get you to answer my DM. Your socials are locked down tighter than Fort Knox."

I took a deep breath, feeling the shift happening right in that moment. "Well, it's time for a change. I'm going public."

Lexi practically vibrated with excitement. "Oh, you're *so* going to blow up. Eric Mann's girlfriend *and* on the PR list for Lexi & Tegan skincare after the viral video? The internet is gonna lose it."

Felicia grinned. "From foe to friend. It's perfect."

Brody lifted his cappuccino. "Let's coffee-cheer to new beginnings."

"To new beginnings."

We clinked our mugs, sipping in unison, the air electric with excitement.

Then Felicia cleared her throat, her eyes sparkling like she'd been sitting on a secret too big to contain. "Speaking of new beginnings... I have news."

We all turned to her, waiting.

"You know how I've been relying on Eva for rides since I haven't replaced my car?"

I nodded. All too aware.

She hesitated for just a second, then broke into a grin. "Well, I've been keeping a little secret. Instead of buying a new car, I've been saving that money. And... *I bought the café*!"

My jaw dropped. "Wait—what?!"

"Guy was selling it, and I convinced him to wait until I had a down payment ready. We made the deal two years ago... and now it's official. Desert Bloom belongs to us, Eva. We're business partners!"

I gasped, my heart pounding like I'd just run a marathon. "We are?"

Felicia beamed. "To new beginnings."

We raised our mugs again, and this time, it really felt like the start of something incredible.

Please turn the page for a sneak peek

into Girl Fight Series book 4

AUTUMN FALLING

available now.

AUTUMN FALLING

Girl Fight Book 3

CHAPTER

ONE

KNEAD, KNEAD, KNEAD. REPEAT.

The air was 90% butter at this point—if I lit a match, the whole café would've gone up in a flambé of frustration. Dawn hadn't just broken; it had tripped and face-planted into the window, casting a pathetic gray glow over the countertops. My eyelids sagged like sandy balloons. I wasn't built for mornings like this. My body still thought it was 2 a.m., itching for a bad taco stand and a tummy ache of *regret*.

Felicia, meanwhile, was thriving. She pirouetted around the kitchen like Ina Garten on espresso, tarts and muffins emerging from the oven as if by magic—golden, flaky, and smugly perfect. I half-expected them to wink at me.

Then it hit me: this wasn't Guy's café anymore. It was *ours*. The realization hit like a rogue baguette to the face. I kneaded at the dough like it signed my paychecks, praying it'd morph into something that didn't resemble a fossilized pancake.

"You're nailing it," Felicia chirped, though her side-eye screamed "I've seen toddlers with better motor skills."

I wished I shared her delusion. Seven attempts. Seven disasters. Attempt 1) a crumbly mess that could've doubled as sand art. Attempt 2) a soggy blob that even the café's resident mouse (RIP, Keith) would've side-eyed. Attempt 3) over-kneaded into a rubbery brick. "Eva, gluten's a rule, not a suggestion," Felicia had sighed, as if I'd insulted her entire ancestry.

I'd nodded solemnly, like I hadn't spent weeks over-kneading my *entire life* into a sad, stretchy mess. My existence was basically a gluten-free pretzel at this point—all the effort, none of the structure.

"That's what you said when I burned the croissants," I muttered, blowing flour off my nose. I looked less "artisan baker" and more "Puritan ghost who'd died mid-bake-off." The white powder coated everything—my apron, my hair, *my will to live*.

And the worst part? I still couldn't wrap my head around how I'd gone from "Eva enjoys Saturday cortados by the window table" to "Eva, co-owner of a café she's one bad batch away from torching." Life had become a whirlwind, all right. And not the fun kind.

Felicia had executed the con of the century, and I'd been about as observant as a potted plant. For two years, she'd played me like a fiddle, cozying up to Guy—the café's former owner—like a Bond villain negotiating world domination. Month by month, she'd funneled cash into a secret "Buy the Café" fund, sacrificing what I can only assume was her entire shoe budget *and* her will to live. And Guy? That sly old fox had pocketed the cash, tossed her the keys, and bolted to a retirement village where his biggest daily challenge was now beating Mildred at bingo. Meanwhile, our lattes were still funding his shuffleboard habit.

We'd officially become "business owners" three weeks ago. Felicia was thriving, buzzing around like she'd been mainlining espresso since birth. Me? I was one misplaced muffin away from a full existential meltdown. I wanted to be useful—really!—but after two weeks of botching orders and accidentally switching out oat milk for non-fat, I'd been demoted to... *baking*.

Ah, baking. My true calling—if my calling involved dough that could double as hockey pucks and a soufflé that sighed like a disappointed parent. My medical (*pfft*) career? Useless here, unless someone needed a PowerPoint on why over-kneading causes carpal tunnel.

Next up: the coffee machine. A foolproof plan! Except the La Marzocco took one look at me and went full *Exorcist*, spewing grounds like it was auditioning for a horror film. Felicia, ever the cheerleader, suggested I "ease in" with the Mastrena instead. That relic shuddered like it was having a midlife crisis, and she yanked the plug before it could yeet itself into the afterlife. "It's never done that before!" she cried, sweat beading on her brow.

"It's not that I don't trust you with the machines," Felicia said later, in a tone that screamed "I'd trust a toddler with a chainsaw first." "It's just... maybe stick to... measuring things?"

So here I was, elbow-deep in flour, channeling my inner Ina Garten while secretly wondering if "home baking experience" was code for "once burned toast and cried." Felicia hovered nearby, her smile strained as she mentally tallied the cost of my sixth failed crust attempt. "You'll get the hang of it!" she said, with the forced optimism of someone watching their life savings evaporate in butter.

We both knew the truth: if I kept this up, we'd be recouping losses by selling my "artisanal" dough bricks as doorstops.

"What if I stick to *not* baking?" I blurted, wedging myself between the oven and the fridge like a human panic attack. The kitchen had shrunk to the size of a shoebox, and I was pretty sure the walls were judging me. A tiny voice in my head hissed, "You're hemorrhaging butter money, Eva!" but I drowned it out.

Felicia sighed like a disappointed teacher, flour drifting off her apron like confetti at a very sad party. "Eva, sweetie, you're a *co-owner* now. You can't just… chill."

I slumped against the counter, my energy levels rivaling a sloth on melatonin. "It'd be easier to 'chill' if I hadn't been ambushed by this whole 'surprise, you're a business mogul' plot twist. I'm still waiting for the tutorial level!"

It wasn't just the secret café coup. It was the *financial carnage* she'd hidden until the last minute—maxed-out credit cards, drained savings, and a spreadsheet that looked like a horror movie budget. Suddenly, my life savings were less "retirement fund" and more "desperation fund."

"At least Lexi's got her sugar daddy bankrolling her existential crisis," I grumbled. "I've got… this." I gestured to my dried out dough.

Felicia, ever the optimist, insisted fear was "counterproductive." "Leaping blindly builds character!" she'd declared, as if we were starring in a motivational poster titled "BossBabe: A Cautionary Tale."

Truthfully, I'd fantasized about quitting my soul-sucking medical job for years—usually during meetings about paperclip procurement or angry patient protocol. The café was my escape hatch, my fresh start, my… oh god, why is this pie crust *sweating*?

"It's not rocket science," Felicia said, poking my dough like an EOD bomb expert.

"No, it's worse," I snapped. "Rocket scientists don't have to worry about gluten tantrums!"

Felicia finally had enough and snatched the dough from my hands, transforming it into actual pie crusts with the precision of a pastry wizard. I stood there, coated in flour and inadequacy, feeling about as useful as a sentient breadcrumb. Her hands danced over the dough—graceful, practiced, infuriating—while mine still struggled with the concept of "knead, don't murder."

Somewhere beyond my existential crisis, the café door

jingled. My heart rate spiked faster than Felicia's eyebrow.

"Eric's here," she muttered, in a tone full of frustration. He'd become a *frequent flier* at the café lately, popping in for "just a coffee" (it was never just a coffee). I lived for it. Felicia? She'd sooner adopt a feral cat.

I frantically swiped flour off my apron, which only made me look like I'd lost a fight with a ghost, and fluffed my hair into something resembling "I tried."

"We're *closed*," I announced, leaning against the counter with faux professionalism. "Health code violation. Rogue yeast epidemic. It's tragic, really."

He kept advancing, all smirks and biceps and *good lord, how do sweats look that illegal?* His grin was a lethal combo of boyish charm and "I know exactly what you're thinking."

"Perfect," he said, closing the gap between us like a man on a mission.

Before I could squeak "public decency laws!", he hoisted me up, and I instinctively clamped my legs around his waist. His lips met mine, soft and warm and *oh hello, serotonin.* Being petite had its perks—like spontaneous airborne kisses.

I tangled my fingers in his hair, which was unfairly silky for someone who spent 90% of his time punching bags, and stole another kiss. When he finally set me down, his hands lingered on my hips like they'd found their forever home. Letting myself *like* him—let alone *slobber* him—had taken approximately 47 years of therapy (and one mortifying viral video involving Tegan, a wayward "disgusting pig" comment, and a very confused Eric). But here we were.

Progress.

Hot, sweaty, possibly *indecent* progress.

He pulled me into a hug that could've doubled as a bear trap, his voice a low rumble in my ear about missing me, thinking about me mid-kickboxing, and *wouldn't a weekend getaway be nice?* His hands slid under my apron, tracing my spine like he was memorizing it for an exam.

"For the love of god, get a room!" Felicia barked, storming in with the energy of a disapproving nun. "Some of us are trying to run a business here, not star in a softcore baking show."

"That's the plan," Eric fired back, grinning as he laced his fingers through mine. His thumb brushed my palm, sparking a shiver that could've powered the café's espresso machine.

He was joking.

Mostly.

Eric and I had officially entered the "Will They/Won't They" phase of our relationship—a rom-com trope so cliché, even Netflix would've rolled its eyes. Sure, we'd established that we were, biologically speaking, *extremely* compatible. But actual *full-body togetherness*? That required navigating my anxiety and a "slow burn" pace that would've made Jane Austen yell, "Get on with it!"

Painfully slow, if you will.

Honestly, I wasn't sure if I was savoring the tension or just emotionally stalling. (Translation: Why not both?) Watching him unravel was delightful—the way his jaw twitched when I "accidentally" grazed his neck, the way his hands flexed like he was mentally measuring the nearest horizontal surface. And the touching? Soft, teasing strokes that left me vibrating like a poorly balanced washing machine.

"Eva?"

Felicia's voice sliced through my X-rated daydream like a nun with a ruler.

"Hmm?" I croaked, fanning myself with a menu. "Is it just me, or is it *sweltering* in here?"

"I said," Felicia deadpanned, "Lexi and Tegan called an emergency PR meeting. Tomorrow. They want us to 'consult' on their new product launch."

I blinked. "Why? We're in the PR list, not their PR

team." (Last week, their *very important* meeting had been a series of back and forth between Tegan and Lexi that had amounted to, let's see—two plus two equals—nothing!) Plus, Eric's "weekend getaway" idea was sounding far more appealing than playing focus group to Lexi's chaos.

Felicia smirked. "Obviously, this is about Tegan's divorce. The Subreddit's blowing up—Scott's in Phuket with some 'yoga instructor' who's definitely a CIA spy," she said, tossing Eric a cookie like she was feeding a zoo animal. He'd mastered the art of existing near our gossip—hovering silently, snacking stoically, pretending not to know Charles once tried to trademark "Broody McAbs" as a cologne.

"But Tegan's divorcing Scott!" I protested. "Why does she care if he's flirting with a CIA spy?"

"Because pride," Felicia said, as if that explained everything. "And Charles is now undercover as Scott's 'ride or die' to trick him into getting arrested for tax fraud. All to win Lexi back."

I jerked upright. "What the hell are you on about? I didn't hear *any* of this."

Felicia rolled her eyes. "Obviously not. You've been too busy mentally undressing Eric in every conceivable location —the stockroom, the walk-in freezer, the *out of order* bathroom—"

"I have not!" I squeaked, my face flaming hotter than a Cheeto.

I risked a glance at Eric behind the counter, who was now leaning against the espresso machine, casually demolishing a cookie with a smirk that screamed "Liar, liar, apron on fire."

"Just bang him already!" Felicia bellowed, like a Shakespearean herald announcing a royal decree. "You've been about as useful as a decaf espresso since he started giving you those *looks*. Eric, since you're eavesdropping like a TMZ reporter—do the world a favor and put us all out of our misery. Most of all, Eva. Please."

Eric prowled over, his gaze locked on mine like a heat-seeking missile. "Anytime," he purred, voice smoother than a triple-shot latte. Then he winked—*the audacity*—and I knew he couldn't wait until I caved or spontaneously combusted. Whichever came first.

I bit back a grin, my cheeks now matching the café's emergency exit sign. "Can we *not* act like we're filming *Naked Attraction*? Some of us have jobs to get to!"

"Fine," Felicia huffed, slamming a palm onto the counter. "Let's talk budgets. Thrilling, I know."

Eric dipped down, brushing a kiss against my lips so soft I nearly forgot my own name. "Too good to be true," he murmured, pulling back just enough to make my knees wobble. "Call you later."

"Later," I breathed, swaying slightly as he left.

Felicia snapped her fingers in front of my face. "Focus! We're hemorrhaging money faster than Lexi burns through shoes. Guy's tarts funded his retirement villa, and our 'viral fame' lasted about as long as a Snapchat streak."

I groaned. "I told you hashtags aren't a business plan."

"What if we make another viral video?" Felicia said, waving a whisk like a magic wand. "You know… shirtless firemen? Puppies in aprons? Something?"

Suddenly, my old lifeguard-and-bottle-service hustler brain sparked. "What if we host a UFC meet-and-greet? Eric and his buddies, signing autographs… in tank tops?"

Felicia froze, her eyes widening like she'd just spotted a unicorn. "Genius. But only if you promise to finally—"

"No."

"Eva, if he agrees to this, you owe it to humanity to climb that man like a *tree*."

I choked on my laugh. "Stop!"

"It's basic karma!" she insisted, grinning like the Cheshire Cat. "The universe demands it."

Maybe it does, I thought, biting my lip. *And maybe the*

universe is onto something.

Hi, reader! Thank you for reading my story. I loved getting to know Eva and friends and I hope you loved them too.

If you feel up to it, please sign up to my newsletter! I'm not a spammer, so if you get an email every once in a while when I'm updating on new releases or bonus chapters, then it's something!

Subsribe to Blair's Newsletter

As an indie author, reviews are our lifeline. Please leave a review (if you want to!) on Amazon, Goodreads, or The StoryGraph.

Thank you for supporting me! It means the world.

P.S. Drop a line if you want to be in my ARC Team! Email at: authorblairmonroy@gmail.com.

Books by Blair Monroy

GIRL FIGHT SERIES

Girl Fight

Spring Blues

Summer Storm

Autumn Falling

About the Author

Blair Monroy writes funny rom-coms with memorable characters who love hard and play hard. When not writing, she's hanging out by the pool with rosé in one hand and a book in the other.

Summer Storm is the third book in the Girl Fight series.

IG: @blairmonroyauthor

TikTok: @authorblairmonroy

Email: authorblairmonroy@gmail.com

* 9 7 9 8 3 4 8 5 9 4 9 3 0 *